GOD IS A DOG

LOST & FOUND IN PARIS

michelle a. gabow

Copyright © 2015 Michelle A. Gabow.

All rights reserved. No part of this book may be reproduced, stored, or transmitted by any means—whether auditory, graphic, mechanical, or electronic—without written permission of both publisher and author, except in the case of brief excerpts used in critical articles and reviews. Unauthorized reproduction of any part of this work is illegal and is punishable by law.

ISBN: 978-1-4834-2531-3 (sc)
ISBN: 978-1-4834-2532-0 (hc)
ISBN: 978-1-4834-2530-6 (e)

Library of Congress Control Number: 2015901249

Because of the dynamic nature of the Internet, any web addresses or links contained in this book may have changed since publication and may no longer be valid. The views expressed in this work are solely those of the author and do not necessarily reflect the views of the publisher, and the publisher hereby disclaims any responsibility for them.

Any people depicted in stock imagery provided by Thinkstock are models, and such images are being used for illustrative purposes only. Certain stock imagery © Thinkstock.

Lulu Publishing Services rev. date: 3/31/2015

"Joyful, joyful, joyful,
as only dogs know how to be happy
with only the autonomy
of their shameless spirit."
—Pablo Neruda

"I think about walks with the dog as walks
with the integrated self, a self better able to
connect with others and the world."
—Sharon Howell

CONTENTS

Foreword ix

Acknowledgments xiii

1. Stan 1
2. Dubrovka from Dubrovnik 12
3. Film on Pause 15
4. Strange Bread Crumbs 20
5. If Not Now… 23
6. The Truth about Barry and Marc 32
7. A Question of Purpose 35
8. Chien, Le Chien 40
9. Isabella et Karin, A Love Story 50
10. Coup de Foudre 56
11. Zero 64
12. Behind the Velvet Curtain 65
13. The Human Heart 70
14. The Pink Lady Speaks English 74
15. Jules et Jim 81

About the Author 101

FOREWORD

IN THE SUMMER OF 2011, Michelle Gabow and I were living on rue de Douai, a block and a half from the Moulin Rouge. Every morning, she walked to Le P'tit Douai, the café on our corner, to drink *cafe crème* and write longhand until the *serveuse* Marie politely suggested that it was time to make space for the lunch crowd.

Michelle is a playwright, but before she left for Paris, she felt compelled to write about some dogs she met in her neighborhood: Jamaica Plain dogs and the women who owned them. Of course, Paris was filled with women and their dogs, interspecies pairs oozing mystery, tragedy, long-term partnership, and love at first sight—*coup de foudre*. Parisian canine fashion statements included little jackets with black ruffles, chrome and leather leashes, and haute grooming that reflected their owner's hairdos. There were dogs who stretched their leashes taut, others who hung close to their women, and still others who lagged behind, requiring constant tugging. Some dogs strategically paced between two women, and on rainy days, women huddled under umbrellas with lap dogs tucked under their arms. Needless to say, once Michelle arrived in Paris, instead of writing a play, she wrote this collection of short stories.

Many afternoons, I walked through our neighborhood alone, soaking in Paris, and several times, I spotted a dog in the street that made an impression on me. I'd come home and describe these dogs to Michelle, and within a week, they'd appear in a story. In the case of Henri, she wrote about me, too, so now I can honestly say that one of Michelle's fictional characters wrote this foreword to her book. Because in that story, "A Question of Purpose," Henri came to represent the lesson Paris was teaching us that summer: to follow your life instead of trying to make something happen.

Once Michelle had written three or four stories, I noticed a strange phenomenon in our neighborhood. It seemed that the number of woman-dog pairs was markedly increasing. Some mornings, there was a small parade of them prancing down the rue Blanche. If I hadn't known better, I'd swear that somehow word had gotten out and the women on our street were acquiring dogs so they could audition for *God Is a Dog*. They say we are all one, that our brains communicate to each other through invisible electromagnetic networks, so why not? The Paris dog-woman community proliferated, and Michelle picked up their high-pitched conversations.

So take a table at Le P'tit, and step into the private lives of these women and their dogs. Experiencing the elegance of their relationships, the secrets kept faithfully between them, the tenderness of their separations, and the uncanniness of their connections is to revel in Paris life.

Ellen Balis

ACKNOWLEDGMENTS

IT TAKES A COMMUNITY TO live a rich, blessed, and sometimes even charmed life as a woman, lesbian, human being, teacher, and creative artist. Here are just some of the people who make it possible for me every day, listed with profound appreciation for their love, inspiration, protection, encouragement, and support. Thank you:

- All the characters and their dogs that walked into my life, both in the real world and the world of the imagination.
- Ellen Balis, my writing partner and muse, who helped me realize a lifelong dream of writing in Paris and fostered adventures, new Paris friendships, and stories I could never even dream living as part of my life in my sixties.

- Susan Wilbur, my first editor, friend of forty years, and regular movie partner, whose energy and belief in the stories consistently gave me hope and courage.
- Nan Stromberg, who rolled down her window next to mine at a J. P. gas station and screamed, "I can't get *Chien, Le Chien* out of my head. We must have a soiree at our house so you can read your stories!" She, Marcia Fowler, Berit Pratt, and Betsy Smith (my dear, dear friend and brilliant conversationalist) provided a wonderful, cozy space, great people, and a Parisian spread of delights fit for the pickiest of French food connoisseurs.
- My amazing friends Dede Ketover and Nancy Carlucci, who literally transformed my life as a playwright by energetically believing in me in my thirties and producing most of my plays for more than thirty years. Thank you for also providing a beautiful community church space, Wellfleet Preservation Hall, for my second reading of *God Is a Dog: Lost and Found in Paris* to a surprisingly large audience (thanks to their publicity) for an unpublished book reading, and whose sumptuous beef brisket and coconut cake has made each Rosh Hashanah a memorable occasion with family. Thanks to Diane Goss, Pam Hall, Laura Hubbard, and Jillian Guerra, who trekked all the way from Boston for that reading.
- Sharon Cox, community activist, poet, philosopher (the first and trusted reader of *all* my work) and Nancy Hughes, teacher, screenwriter; they are my writing group and two of the most brilliant, courageous, and inspiring writers I know.

- Sharon Locke, whose spirit, visual art, and love of the creative process keeps me alive. Michael Baxter, an incredible musician and composer, and Sander Kramer, my beloved "brothers-oudda-law" who add excitement, creativity, and play into my life. Melanie Berzon, my Jewish soul sister who provided the music for all my earlier plays and is a wonderfully creative radio artist. Judy Pomerantz, whose humor and heart has carried me through the hardest of times. Debbie Lubarr, social activist and compassionate teacher who teaches me that change, inside and out, is possible. Joanne O'Neil, who lets me read to her up at the studio at Welcome Hill every summer over several glasses of red wine and "sacred" conversations. Ann Stokes, who has created affordable, breathtaking studio space at Welcome Hill for women artists. Amy Mandel for her gentle spirit and courage. Myra Hindus, who provides therapy and love over many dinners in Jamaica Plain. Shani Dowd for her belief in my work and her long-term friendship. Doug Mcleod, who shared and encouraged our lives in Paris. Paula Gallitano, composer and musician, and the rebirth of our close, heartfelt friendship. Iren Handschuh, a visual visionary. Paul Walrond (S. K.), just because we believe in each other. John Selig, my second proofreader (a unique combination of thoroughness and thoughtfulness). Marisa Hollinshead for her technical support and open spirit. A Jamaica Plain neighbor I met at J. P. Licks one morning over a cup of coffee, who inspired the first story by her own story about her father.

- Warren Gabow and Martha Gabow, my loving family. My mother, Tibie Gabow, and my dad, Moish Gabow, who would have loved these stories. My cousin Tina Weinraub, just for being Tina.
- Diane Goss and Jane Adellizzi ("the girls"), two amazing teachers, writers, and thinkers. My students, who teach me important life lessons every day and give me hope. The PAL faculty at Curry College (many of whom have attended nearly all my plays). All my friends who supported me in countless ways, believed and encouraged me from the vey beginning, audienced my plays, were on the many boards of *Hysterical Performances*, and are too numerous to put on these pages but change my life every day in every way.
- Our cat, Stella, and our Yorkie, Stanley, who is the inspiration for all these stories.
- Most of all, my deepest appreciation, heart, and thanks I give to Michelle A. Baxter, the love of my life for thirty and then some years, creative partner and edgy director of nearly all my plays. Her inspiration, kindness, compassion for others, passion for social justice, conversations (which we never run out of), sense of humor when I thought there was none left in my life, spirit, and soul has transformed and rocked my world.

STAN

"When morning comes to Morgantown
The merchants roll their awnings down
The milkjocks make their morning rounds
In morning, Morgan..."

OH SHIT, I'M SINGING A damn Joni Mitchell song. Loudly. In the streets. I need a cup of coffee. Now! And to make matters even worse, Stanley just turned his head and smirked at me. Yes, dogs can smirk. Stanley often gives that annoyed glare, bordering on belligerent glare, especially when he decides not to move. He puts on the brakes and smirks. There is absolutely nothing I can do to convince him to budge. This is why we do not take Stan on long walks; it simply isn't pleasant.

MICHELLE A. GABOW

Some people might say that my first encounter with Stan was providence, destiny, fate. I'm more prone to *accident* myself. However, the day after Yom Kippur, my fiery friend Dede and I went to a movie and then to the MSPCA-Angell. I was deeply missing my poor dead Rita, who was an angel of a dog, and I desperately needed a dog fix. Dede understood and drove me there immediately; there's nothing like a friend who gets you.

The MSPCA was closed, for some odd reason. I jiggled the front entry door and strongly shook it again. Before I knew it, I was banging at the door over and over, until I noticed Dede's stricken face. "We'll come back tomorrow," she said gently. I was livid, crazy. Or was it depressed? Depression had settled in comfortably during this whole sabbatical break, and being denied access to some stray, lonely dogs had just nailed it into place.

Just as we were about to leave the parking lot, we heard a voice screaming from a car. "Dog... dog... *perro*... dog!" An older man and a young girl rushed toward us. She had what seemed to be a baby wrapped in a blanket, wrapped in her arms. Of course it was a very small dog, Chester, who eventually morphed into our Stanley. She begged us to adopt him, said she and her grandfather drove all the way from New Hampshire, showed us his pedigree papers. He was so perfect. In spite of this—or maybe because of this—I became temporarily mute. Dede leaped right in and proceeded to ask the vital questions to this young woman. Her grandfather only spoke Spanish.

"Why are you giving him up?"

The young girl said that she was going to college in California, but somehow, when pressed, she couldn't recall which school it was.

"How old is Chester?"

Four years old, and to that, the girl added that Chester had been abused. Later, we discovered through his papers and shots that she only had him for one month.

My partner Michelle's only requests for the next dog I happened upon—because she knew it was only a matter of time—were minimal: first, that she not be white (every dog we had owned was white); and second, that she be medium-sized. She wanted a *dog* dog, an animal with stature that she could walk proudly in the streets. That's what made me finally blurt out a question.

"Will he grow?"

The girl just looked at me blankly, like I was some kind of fool she might want to reconsider as a potential dog-parent, and sardonically reiterated, "He's a Yorkshire terrier."

Dede, who remained in control and on top of the situation, asked the final question: "Was Chester house-trained?"

Now, if we weren't both already smitten, we would have noticed the long pause on the girl's part. That, and the fact that the grandfather seemed to suddenly recover his English comprehension. "Yes," was his response.

If his yes meant "not a chance, no way, not ever, don't hold your breath", then the grandfather was right. Our absolutely adorable Yorkshire terrier released any and all food, water, and other unknown substances from each orifice of his skeletal little body on every chair, bedspread, carpet, throw rug, table leg, radiator, sneaker, trash basket, and doorframe in the teeny, rented apartment we call home.

For days…

Weeks...

Months.

Although completely in love with me, he growled under his breath every time Michelle approached him and overtly every time she approached me. Needless to say, this was a strain on our relationship.

The poor boy was barely able to eat or chew, choked feverishly as if it was his last breath when he sipped any water, and viciously attacked all dogs larger or smaller than himself. He was seven pounds of pure hell.

One would ask, and I'm sure you're thinking, "Why the hell didn't these ladies take him back to the pound?" And all I can say to that completely logical question is that if nothing else, what Stan had was possibilities. We just had to somehow discover and remove the rock this potential crawled under; it was our own search-and-destroy mission.

Although walking Stanley was like walking a turtle, not only in size but also in his stop-and-go pace, there were small, sometimes almost imperceptible miracles happening inside our apartment. It took me a few months to realize that the level of poop and pee in the house had, in fact, decreased 75 percent! And that Michelle was able to occasionally pet Stan without a growl on either part. One day, while I was at work (of course), Stan licked Michelle while she was lying on the sofa, cried to join her, and proceeded to fall asleep on her chest. From that day on, he no longer completely ignored Michelle when she came in the door. Perhaps it was not the castrato greeting and circle dance I would get, but it was a notable wag of the tail from a distance. I knew her personal opera was close at hand.

GOD IS A DOG

There were also street delights with Stan. Bus drivers, primarily women, for some reason, would stop their buses and open the passenger doors just to coo about Stan.

"Perfect for my grandson or my daughter or the city."

"I just had to stop and admire him."

"What kind of dog is that?"

"What's his name?"

And when I would reply "Stanley," they would beam from ear to ear. Strangers would walk past him and laugh out loud. Stan was a hit; but more than that, the audacious swagger of the tail, the crop of his head and left ear when he was curious, and his bowlegged strut was a smile. A smile I so desperately needed.

Today, I thought, Stanley and I would do a little experiment. We would check out a neighborhood outdoor café and see if he could be civil through a chocolate croissant and café au lait. So, what was usually a brisk twenty minute walk resulted in a forty-five minute exploration of every new pole, wall, tree, blade of grass: sniff and pee, sniff and pee. A walk with double the pauses for exercise. I refused to be exasperated and used the time to contemplate my sabbatical—or, to put it bluntly, my four months in bed.

Everything that I so carefully arranged for the sabbatical fell apart. The *unplanning* of me rattled my insides. Fear, my most fervent antagonist, lived large and big. Leaving the house was a huge push, and only Stan could get me into the sun, because during that time, even the sun hurt—a sting I could feel for days. My two-month trip to Paris, a lifelong dream, was a gift to myself to celebrate my completed chapters of a book of letters that never happened. The young man who stole my car one cold November day two years ago wrote the most thoughtful and provocative

5

letters from jail (a story which itself needs to be told). He disappeared when he was released, only to return to my doorstep at the end of May. In my state of mind and body lethargy, this was probably a good thing. But in three days' time, I was going straight from my bed to Paris.

This walk to the café was crucial; I needed to test the Paris waters. Stan kept me engaged, steady on the busy street and slowed down. The fact that I suddenly found myself singing loudly in the middle of a bustling Centre Street was a sign that my courage just might be creeping back. The sun, the sound of traffic, a destination, suddenly felt good, damn good.

***

I am liking this walk. This thinking and not thinking. This breath. This pace. The sun doesn't burn as much. Maybe I'm even happy—or at least, content. I am in no hurry. Stan can sniff and pee to his heart's desire. I do not beg him to move when he puts on the brakes. We have no arguments in the middle of the street today. It is perfect. We are perfect.

"Mornin' Morgantown…"

Whoops.

Stanley decides to lie down in the middle of the sidewalk. *Is it my singing or the long walk?* I wonder. I calmly and softly tell him, "We're almost there"—like that helps. I carry him to some steps that lead to one of the rare well-maintained Jamaica Plain housing developments that is set back on a hill, and we sit. As soon as we sit, Stan is ready for action, tail wagging like mad, little *ooffs* from deep in his throat, his eyes searing my soul. I am not in control today. And that's just fine with me.

GOD IS A DOG

"When morni—"

Jesus!

The second half of the walk has a steadier pace. Stan's *mojo* has come back fully and passers-by are all smiles. There is a strut to our walk, like I am a person with a real *dog* dog. Stan has taken a day off from his vicious attacks on other dogs. We are both, in our own way, appreciating J. P., a diverse inner-city Boston neighborhood that has a small-village feel and a sizable population of transgender, gay, and lesbian artists; dogs; cafes; and activists; it's the place I've lived for most of my adult life.

We are quickly approaching the block of J. P. Licks, our café destination, and obedience issues aside, something is off-balance. My body keeps tilting toward the edge of the sidewalk and leaning perilously close into incoming traffic. This only comes to my attention when Stanley jerks me back into the middle. I am a little shaken when suddenly, I reach up to my right ear and notice that my favorite silver hanging earring is gone. These are the earrings I will be wearing on the plane to Paris. These are my courage earrings. My good luck earrings. An early birthday gift from Michelle. I love these earrings. This is not something to take lightly. I try not to panic by panicking, searching my scarf, my hair, the inside of my T-shirt, literally feeling myself up in the middle of a busy street. But I don't care. I am determined. My earring is not lost. I retrace my steps. But Stanley isn't having any of this. He puts on the brakes hard. I end up dragging him over the pavement. Our battle is becoming an undeclared war.

"Shit." The word keeps escaping from my mouth.

"Shit." I search the poles, the doorways, cracks in the sidewalk, newly planted small trees.

7

MICHELLE A. GABOW

"Shit."

Car tires, The Same Old Place, The Smoke Shop, Verizon.

"Shit, shit, shit…"

City Feed, back and forth, back and forth, to no avail. The smell of freshly made pizza from The Same Old is making me a little nauseous. *I will not vomit. I will not vomit.* Stanley whimpers. And he's not the only one. Tears plummet down my cheeks.

Out of the corner of my bleary, bloodshot eyes, I notice a woman on the dark steps between Verizon and City Feed Café. She is signaling to all walkers, with her fingerless wool gloves (in summer) making a "come hither" motion. As she tips the palm of her hand and forefinger in her gesture, her begging has a sexual nuance, but few people bother to give her their change. Stanley, who is not the friendliest dog in the world, is unexpectedly drawn to her and pulls me toward the steps. Although I haven't given up on the earring waiting for me somewhere in the vicinity, I'm just too damn tired to pull back.

As we approach the steps, the sitting woman grabs her broken down black purse and holds it close to her breasts. I sit, exhausted and out of breath. The doorway smells of stale cigarettes, body odor and pee. I am not sure if it's me and my anxiety, the steps, or the woman. Tears are slowly evaporating, but I can feel my swollen lids and the red, blotchy patches on my face. Carefully, the woman places her left hand to block the breeze in front of her cigarette lighter and lights her cigarette on the first try. I'm impressed.

I notice, even through my own haze, that her body is tight and compact. She could be anywhere from thirty to fifty years old. Her skin is the color of eggplant with a warm violet tone below her high cheekbones. She is still looking into the street, as if expecting a package delivery. The hanging cigarette droops from her mouth. She's that "don't mess with me" kind of tough. However, Stanley, my abused dog who is terrified of friends and strangers alike, jumps right into her lap. I am stunned. My jaw opens like a cartoon character. She somehow manages to smile at Stan with the cigarette still hanging from her lips, which is both beautiful and incongruous at the same time.

I am her elder but I feel like a child. She strokes Stanley with such gentleness and compassion that my eyes begin to water all over again. She looks at me, and her deep brown eyes swallow me up. She waits for me to say something. I can't talk. We sit silently for a few moments.

Then I blurt out, "I lost my favorite earring," and start to bawl like a baby. "I'm sorry. I'm sorry. I..."

I am a blithering idiot. She is still smoking.

Then I begin my monologue between fits of sniveling hysterics. "Excuse me, but women in their sixties do not take fits in doorways," I inform my new friend.

She takes another drag, a long one.

"But I'm losing everything. Everything! Do you have any idea what that's like?"

She seems to have an idea.

"I rarely misplace anything, but since October, I lost my paycheck—twice—my wallet, my datebook. It's amazing that I haven't lost Stan. My keys, at least seven times, the most perfect jean jacket, at least a half a dozen socks, my mom, several pairs of sunglasses, countless lipsticks, twenty pairs of reading glasses, my dog Rita, a fountain pen, sweaters, gloves, hats, my favorite earrings that Michelle bought me when... my mom..."

Okay, now I'm weeping. Stanley moves between us. He jerks his head oddly to the left. He is perfectly still and does not take his eyes off of me. It is more attention than I can bear. My insides are on fire—yet, I can't stop talking. And crying. The odd thing is, people don't notice us as they pass by, or they pretend not to notice. We are all invisible. Ghosts in the alcove.

"Today is Friday," I go on. "Friday. I take Mom to the hairdressers right in the Hebrew Rehab. Will she be rageful, screaming 'fuck you' to all the nurses, or too doped up to pick up her head; funny and satirical, telling me that God sent me today, or brutal to other residents, especially Esther; crying because my father, who died ten years ago, is now 'sleeping with his girlfriend in a brand new king size bed across the hall;' obsessing on my being too early or too late; hysterically laughing? Will she remember me today? Does she need her outfit laid out, a slice of pizza for lunch, a chocolate donut? What do I do now?"

The woman holds out an empty pack of Marlboro Lights and moves her head toward the smoke shop. It's an order and feels all too familiar. Besides, it's the least I can do. I leave Stan with her but he is still totally watching my every move. I buy two packs and a lighter.

Stan wags his tail and sings his opera when I return, as if I were away for a year. The woman laughs from the belly, a laugh that is energetic and full of heart. I realize this is not only the first time I hear her laugh, but it is the first sound that comes out of her mouth. I light two cigarettes and give her one—a real Bette Davis, *Now, Voyager* moment. I make a joke.

"Why ask for the moon when we have the stars?"

She doesn't get it.

We sit in our doorway, smoking our cigarettes. In complete silence. I am a wrung out dishtowel, awake, burned to the core, light, all at once. She is, too. I know this. Someone comes close to us; Stan snarls under his breath and then viciously barks. The man retreats.

A smoker's deep, sexy, hoarse voice echoes in our small entryway.

"Oddiza dojji."

Oh, shit! My friend doesn't speak English. How did I not notice? What a self-centered asshole I am. In the middle of my personal diatribe, she beckons me with her gloveless forefinger to come closer. Stan and I scoot over on the step. She kisses his head. After the kiss, she cups her hands and rests her lips between them, dangerously close to my right ear. The stench of cigarette and whiskey is overwhelming, as she eloquently and briefly reiterates, "God is a *d-o-g.*"

Instantly, the woman with violet skin and wool fingerless gloves transforms back into character and resumes her necessary performance.

DUBROVKA FROM DUBROVNIK

IRPORTS ARE COLD PLACES, EVEN when the weather is warm, which at the moment, Dublin is not. Not a dog in sight. I'm looking—searching, really. For Stanley's eyes. Dublin is our stop before Paris. I people watch and listen to all the destination announcements. A flight is announced to Dubrovnik. Just at that instant, my brain switches. I'm remembering my friend, Dubrovka from Dubrovnik, at twenty-two; the two of us sharing Bob Dylan, records she had to hide because of the new government, our thoughts on socialism, and "power to the people."

"Dubrovnik is now boarding."

Where is she now? Where the hell did twenty-two go? We were so thrilled to meet each other. Countries distanced us, but at that moment, *we* were our country. It existed between us. The streets of Dubrovnik and dreams were all ours. We were amazed to find each other, to be such like souls,

GOD IS A DOG

and we talked nonstop. We laughed hysterically at nearly every conversation and then look at each other, surprised, because we always forgot the joke. She's probably married with a family now. Or perhaps she's on her second divorce.

Today, as I sit in the airport waiting for my flight to Paris, I clearly see Dubrovka. It's as if the sound of the name of her country over the loudspeaker has given me a chance to cross barriers again. At this moment in time, I envision the back of her as if I'm several steps behind. Her gait still has that same relaxed, but focused pace up the hills of Dubrovnik. I surprise myself with a smile. I have crossed the ocean yet again, and we meet. My mind opens to her life. It's as real as this airport, my trip to Paris, Michelle sitting across from me reading, and the absence of Stan. She seems to be returning home to an apartment after a long day at work. No, it's not quite an apartment but a small studio. Does she live alone now? It's amazing that at sixty-two, she has changed little. Her long, thick, black hair down to her waist now has a touch of salt, and her once-twenty-two-year-old slim frame is fleshed out in all the right places.

As she turns the key, a few art books drop from her bag. I realize that she, too, is a professor. I remember her love of art history. I now don't only see but feel her, as if I'm there, inside her heart and her mind. She is looking forward to a long cup of coffee in solitude, or as close to solitude as she can get. Suddenly, I possess her recent memory. Darius, her fluffy, longhaired mutt who picked her up on the streets one summer day, greets her at the door, barking in his operatic voice. She jokes with him about being *castrati*, pets him behind his broken ear, and smiles.

13

I don't know at this moment, but can only wonder that just maybe she recalls twenty-two and that young American girl she met who loved Bob Dylan. Maybe, for a fleeting second, she wonders about that brief friendship, as she brews her coffee. We believed we were on the precipice of awareness of ourselves as women of the world.

As Darius, who is definitely larger than a lap dog, jumps on her lap, they both slowly look around the apartment, an apartment she decorated all for herself, with her favorite things and most-loved colors. She surprises herself with a smile, as her eyes take it all in: movie posters of her new favorite, *The Girl Who Played with Fire*, old photos of Djuna Barnes and Gertrude Stein alongside Bob Dylan and Rolling Stones posters. Her room is painted in hot pinks and oranges, a perpetual sunset. Outside her large window are the stone staircases so reflective of Dubrovnik and her life.

"The journey back to me," she whispers in Darius's ear.

The sun is setting inside and outside her flat. A tear drops and Darius quickly kisses her cheeks.

Yes, yes... that's how I see this journey. That's how I see many of our journeys, whether we are alone, or coupled, with dog, or with cat, to this place, where the smile meets the tear.

FILM ON PAUSE

WE ARRIVE IN PARIS, MICHELLE and I, on June 1—the day of our thirtieth anniversary. This is and has been our dream celebration. Michelle will stay one month that includes Paris, Amsterdam with her brother Michael, and Cassis. I hopefully will write for two months in my little apartment in the *neuvième*. Although exhausted from our flight and too much Ativan, we disembark at Charles De Gaulle full of anticipation and romance.

Our apartment is only a train ride and metro away. I can't believe it! *Nous ne pouvons pas le croire!* The more I practice my French, the more believable it is. Our luggage is heavy, but what do we care? Michelle says, "We'll build our arm muscles"—something I've been working on to no avail for months. I am, however, a little sorry that I over-packed; despite them having rollers, or maybe because of the rollers, we have to carry our suitcases up a multitude

MICHELLE A. GABOW

of steps. We are faced with staircases at every turn. They seem to be multiplying before our eyes. It reminds me of the brooms in Disney's *Fantasia*, a movie that gives me nightmares to this day. I can't help but wonder where the hell the escalators are. The heel of my left foot in my beautiful, very flat gladiator sandals is killing me, but I know everything will be fine as soon as I jump into the plush bed and breathe. However, my love, Michelle, keeps misreading the signs, and we go up and down the same staircases in circles, dragging our roller bags, which behave like stubborn mules, behind us.

Finally, we enter our beautiful apartment on the third floor. Third floor, by the way, translates to our American fourth. Even though it doesn't have a view, only windows to a missing courtyard, it is more spacious and absolutely perfect for our romantic adventure. Nevertheless, at this point and after four more flights of stairs with our lovely rollers, we can barely look at each other, let alone have a conversation. Michelle, forever optimistic, finally breaks the uncomfortable silence, deciding that if we can only eat in a French café, nothing else will matter, because after all, we'll be living the dream.

We leave, renewed by these thoughts. I realize, as the door of our apartment locks after us, that I left the door codes to the downstairs door inside our new home. Michelle has already made it to the first floor.

"Wait!" I scream.

She has the gall to say, "What now?"

I don't respond. When I put the key in the keyhole, the fuckin' key won't turn, pardon my French. I call to Michelle to come back upstairs and try the key. I hear her grunting in anger at each step. She, who is mechanically much more

GOD IS A DOG

inclined than I am (truth be told, anyone is), reiterates that it just doesn't work.

At this point, almost like a mirage, this beautiful French lesbian in a motorcycle jacket and helmet comes rushing down the stairs. We stop her and beg for help. Maybe there's a French way of unlocking we know nothing about. She tries the key and looks me right in the eye. I'm ready to chuck everything, including Michelle and our thirty years, and jump right into her bed. She shakes her head and says, "*Non.*" It takes me a second or two to realize she is referring to the key.

Michelle and I are really at a loss; besides the fact that we truly want to kill each other, we have no phone number for our landlords. That, too, is sitting comfortably on our plush bed. We can't leave the building because we don't have the code, and neither of us can really speak French. In all this turmoil, I do get a brainstorm and ask Michelle to find an Internet café. Our landlord's phone number is in my e-mail. We quarrel back and forth for more than a few loud minutes about who will go.

"You can at least speak the language!" she barks.

"But you can do Internet stuff much better than me!" I scream.

This is always true because as I said, anyone can. We go back and forth for what seems like an hour but is only a few minutes. It's true that my stamina for arguing is phenomenal; so I win.

There happens to be a cyber café around the corner, and the landlord returns after Michelle calls. Yes, it's true; the lock is broken. He hints that it may be our fault, and this is when we are finally in unison, with a loud "no way!" He will have to get a locksmith but this will be *très difficile*

17

MICHELLE A. GABOW

because tomorrow, June 2, is some kind of French holiday. He suggests that we pass the time in his favorite restaurant called Le Zebra but fails to tell us the name of the street. According to him, it is easy to find, as it is somewhere up the hill near the Moulin Rouge. We circle the Moulin Rouge for about forty-five minutes, until my heel hurts so much that I decide to go back to our building. Michelle insists on finding a place to eat; after all, it is perfect Parisian weather. The landlord has given me the codes, but he is nowhere to be found and neither is the apartment key.

I march down the stairs, each step stinging my heel and shooting pain to my right shoulder. I make a left out of the building and suddenly see Michelle *avec une bière* at the outdoor café up the street. She looks at me kind of sweetly, waves me over, and then orders us both quiches. We drink our beer in silence.

Across the street, two older women in their eighties or so are walking their respective dogs. One woman has a Yorkshire terrier on her leash, low to the ground, shaggier than most and looking a bit too much like our Stanley. The other woman is walking a dog that resembles our last dog, Rita, a white Coton de Tulear, with blue-black spots. They and their dogs walk slowly. The women are extremely animated, talking loudly first to each other and then to their dogs.

Suddenly, all our eyes lock and it's as if we have set our film on pause. Our six bodies are jolted into our own private time machine. No one moves. No one speaks. No one drinks any beer.

Then, as if a dog whistle went off, the dogs pull the two older women into their natural speed. They push their mistresses into awake, as they simultaneously lift

GOD IS A DOG

their legs to pee, a kind of a salute to the powers that be. I feel an electrical current as Michelle presses her knee to my thigh, as future and past melt into the Parisian sidewalk.

STRANGE BREAD CRUMBS

ONE CAN MARK HER WAY around Paris by homeless domains. Strange bread crumbs. However, people don't just mark their territory; sometimes, they create elaborate spaces and take up residence for entire days and nights. Maybe years. So *homeless* may not be the correct term. My biggest question—besides, of course: How do some of us get to this place?—is: When the hell do they eat or take a piss? And from the looks of things, the latter commences right in their spot. The filth is their protection from pillage and general disturbance. They are Paris's untouchables. So, when Chelle and I find ourselves lost, we find our way like Hansel and Gretel were supposed to, by their bread crumbs.

Some create fantastic, yet filthy beds, lifted up, with odd quilts and clothes for their covers. Some live in barricades of plastic bags and *bagages,* a wagon-train circle of house

GOD IS A DOG

and home. Some find nooks and crannies that could be doorways but are not. Some use each other for their cushions and beds, positioning themselves in perfect *S* shapes, and many more sit and sleep on the hard, dirty cement cushioned only by their layers, as black as night. You almost have to step over the bodies bathed in their own vomit. There is really no way to escape the brutality of Paris streets among the history and riveting architecture. The more populated the area is with tourists, the more dense the population of homeless homes.

Begging is a way of life.

Yet, true artists create the most dramatic of these makeshift abodes. They are homeless women barefoot on the hot Paris pavements, men with bellies that touch the ground when sitting, and young men, who were, at one time, beautiful, with left over smiles of a tooth here and there. They create theatrical scenes, frozen in time. They are part of a band of artists creating frescos, a forgotten art form mirroring forgotten lives. Although these magnificent and horrible pieces are brilliantly arranged and directed, the art world does not sing their praises or write blurbs reflecting how their art form depicts the meaning of Paris life in the present, or find galleries in which to display their controversial work. Their galleries or theaters are their own homes, the inside of their lives for the world of shoppers and sightseers to view. Their characters, and sometimes actors, are alive and real. They are well trained or carefully placed in precise positions. There is no line of demarcation between art, life, and survival.

Today, the red Hop-On, Hop-Off tour bus dropped us just a few feet from one such fresco. Of course, it was not one of the Parisian sights or *histoires* told through our

MICHELLE A. GABOW

plugged-in earphones. It was not the square where Marie Antoinette was beheaded or Napoleon Bonaparte's Grande Palace. It was not the stones taken from the aristocracy during the French Revolution and placed on the streets as a symbolic gesture of the proletariat, and it certainly wasn't Mona Lisa's smile at the Louvre. However, it was located just a few feet from the tour bus's regular stop.

Voila. Just a few steps. We witness the man whose belly touches the pavement. And like any good tourist, I remove my digital pink Canon from its pink case to take a photo. He smiles. It isn't a posed smile or a belligerent smile. He shakes his forefinger.

"Aucun argent, aucune photo."

I had just dished out five euros for the Grande Palais exhibition and twenty-five euros for the tour bus; my plays, though modestly priced, are always at least ten dollars. So, I pay for my admission ticket, and I am poised to take a portrait of him and his amazingly brilliant actors—a brown mutt with round, frameless glasses, his arm/leg gently placed around a gray-and-white cat. Unlike their master, their director, they are both apparently well taken care of and immaculately clean. Both follow the direction to sleep soundly and lovingly amidst the crowd. His heart, non-surgically removed, bleeds for us while his family, exposed on a daily basis to the harsh realities of tourism and Lafayette traffic, sleep like babies in the heart and belly of Paris.

Snap.

IF NOT NOW...

BY NATALIE TERRANOVA

I WANTED A PHOTO OF HER this morning, just at this moment, bare shoulders bursting out of the duvet, cup of coffee in her hand, smiling. Not for the purpose of memory. Not even for the morose reason of capturing her before she became thin with illness. It was just because. Her shoulders were round and strong, and I wanted another excuse to gaze, to revel. At eighty-four, she still had the most delicious shoulders. Believe me, I've had my taste of shoulders in my day.

We made passionate love this morning. Perhaps not with the athleticism, abandonment, or forbearance of our twenties, thirties, or even our early seventies. Yet, our bodies kneaded, baked, and rose as if in the hands of the finest

MICHELLE A. GABOW

artisan *boulanger*. We twisted and braided like delectable croissants, then melted like butter. Damn, I was famished.

"Come on, Marie, get the dogs. We're going out," I announced.

"*Oui,*" she replied. "*Je faim aussi.*"

Words could never articulate how happy I was at that moment. *Mon amour* of fifty years was hungry.

"Starving," I whispered, as I nibbled on her right shoulder.

She giggled like a schoolgirl.

Dressing was always a quick and easy affair for Marie, even now. A tweed skirt reasonably below the knee, a simple black jacket, sensible shoes, a dash of red lipstick, with her blonde (with a little help) coiffure tied in a knot around the nape of her neck. I appreciated Marie's fashion sense: simple, elegant, and English, leaving much to the imagination. I, on the other hand, was her darker Italian sister. Today, I wore a long, black skirt, sensible shoes (a necessity at our age), a black blouse with white pearl buttons, and a Chinese-red flowing jacket. What Marie labeled as my "coat of armor" required the most time: painstakingly chosen bangles and bracelets down each arm, several layers of necklaces and long, gold chains, large, clip-on red earrings, and an assortment of fantastic rings on every finger, including my thumb. My powder and rouge was thick and theatrical, my non-existent eyebrows were painted, and my deep plum lipstick made a luscious (one could say *strong*) statement. My blue-black hair (also from a bottle) was tied in a French knot, similar to Marie's. Two bookends walking our dogs.

"Gertrude, Alice..." It was ridiculous to call them. They were resting in their perspective beds until the last bangle

GOD IS A DOG

sounded. Like a bell, it called them to attention, Alice with both leashes in her mouth, the two of them salivating at the front door. Gertrude might have been the alpha dog; however, Alice was way more than a dutiful wife. She was smart, organized, and always prepared. They both were well aware of their roles and when to break them, not unlike each of their namesakes.

Gertrude was a Yorkshire terrier; low to the ground, and multi-colored, with a little more gray along her snout and eyes. Most Yorkies weigh from seven to nine pounds; our Gertrude beat them all by two pounds. Although round, stomach almost touching the ground, she carried herself with grace and fortitude, forever our leader. She took us through the Paris streets with ease, a new route each time and a new return path. We, at least the two of us, always had a little fear that perhaps we were lost, but we never were. She experimented with routes and we experimented with Paris. Alice, on the other hand, had complete trust in Gertrude, a trust that was never broken.

Alice was a Coton De Tulear, a rare breed originally from Madagascar. She was longhaired, taller than Gertrude (though short in stature), and elegant. Her bright-white fur had black markings, more like clouds on a summer day than spots; she was the sun and the rain to all of us. If it were up to Gertrude, everyone in the streets would be our friend. Alice was a bit more discerning. She kept all of us true to ourselves and somehow living in the truth of real friendship. Gertrude was our eyes and ears; Alice was most definitely our nose.

We had found Gertrude first, running in circles alone around our neighborhood park. We waited and waited, but no owner appeared. We took her photo and plastered

MICHELLE A. GABOW

pictures all over the neighborhood, but nobody got back to us. Marie and I had no intention of keeping her, but fairly quickly, she conquered our hearts. However, Gertrude never became fully Gertrude until Alice came into the picture. They found each other in a small pet store in the *neuvième*. We all would visit every day until it became apparent to the owner, Michel, that she was ours. Michel refused to sell her to any of her other admirers. There was no choice but to acquiesce. Once she was in our apartment, love for all of us blossomed. The house became a home, and we lived in her inspiration.

Perhaps our walks didn't have the lilt they used to. How could they? Once, all four of us could be found literally skipping down the street. But we still had the same thrill as on the day our first walk commenced. It was always the high point of the day. Our feet, in spite of everything, carried us through Gertrude's surprises, and our conversation was always engaging and magnificently circular. That, too, was part of our original attraction: two working class girls talking about books, art, poetry, life, and longings until sometimes three in the morning. We met in the states, at my cosmetics counter at Gimbels in Philadelphia, and knew right away that this was a lifetime friendship. Well, I knew much more. I was well aware of my inclination. After one short vacation in Paris, we were sold. Paris held us in only the ways a woman can. This was the place that we, as lovers, could live and thrive.

Not that we were demonstrative about our love in public. Both of us said that it made it sexier when we returned to the privacy of our home. I'm not sure how true that was. Maybe our proclaimed honesty was fear in disguise. And just maybe we had a reason to be afraid, even in our

GOD IS A DOG

beloved Paris. After all, we did live through much anti-Semitism, much homophobia, and a world war.

Our saving grace in Paris was a group of girls with our same proclivity. Many poetry soirees took place in our small apartment on rue Blanche, where we stayed up into all hours of the night drinking wine, reading poetry, and occasionally sharing a little Mary Jane to entice the spirits. However, the hours were easier on the other girls who did not have to work, being trust-fund babies both large and small. Nearly all of them, except for Bette and Iren, have passed. Too many funerals at this age, and too few soirees.

Oh, but how easily I stray from the subject of this story, the subject being this Thursday morning in early June.

It was one of those magical Parisian mornings where the sun and clouds sang in perfect harmony, the undercurrent of melody was provided by wind instruments and all were orchestrated to perfection. It brought all four of us to a smile as we shut our door to the street. Yes, Gertrude and Alice were capable of dazzling smiles. Isn't every dog? At the very least, *capable?*

I took hold of both leashes this morning. I didn't know why. Alice was usually Marie's anchor. But somehow, even though Marie was quite feisty and let me just verbalize, very sexy this morning, I thought perhaps she needed to lean on me. A little. She did so without the slightest objection. However, Alice kept looking back and giving Marie a check, what we called "the eye." Just in case. It's not only that Alice needed to be needed. It was because she was truly a "sensitive," which is not so rare in dogs, rarer in humans.

We crossed rue Blanche in silence. I stopped at E. Gless, our favorite and closest *pâtisserie,* and bought two croissants *avec beurre,* a bit more expensive but worth every euro.

27

As we followed Gertrude, we chewed in delight. Before I knew it, Marie had eaten half of her croissant. I was elated! Alice's fluffy, white, circular tail was wagging madly. Marie and I laughed; Alice's pleasure was contagious. She was our emotional barometer.

Our Gertrude was on a roll, blazing a completely new path that took us to le Jardin des Tuileries, across the Seine. It was a longer walk than usual. We could all sense Marie's fatigue and her pride. We sat among the Seine sculptures without a word, until we became a sculpture of ourselves reflected on the river. Each of us was well aware that our return would be by the 74 bus. But for now, we were lit, as if in a Goddard film, by the beauty of everything we loved about Paris.

When Marie caught her breath, she began a conversation about an American film we saw last night, *An Invisible Sign*. Films, especially what Americans call *independent movies*, were not only a magnificent obsession but also provided a panoramic backdrop to our own visions and parallel lives. Although we were not artists, it was our art form, along with poetry, plays, and short stories, art we could take a bite out of and feel satiated.

Marie quickly became highly animated, painting the film with her long, slim fingers in the air as she spoke. Sometimes, the films we saw and discussed were an expression of our differences, and heated arguments would ensue into the early morning hours. Today, it narrated a slice of our own story.

"I love the way numbers appeared in the film, invisible directions, truth-tellers. Just popped up in the air. Voila!"

"*Oui,* our life has been like that, our love story," I responded.

GOD IS A DOG

"But the signs were visible. Coming to the make-up counter at Gimbels for my usual red lipstick and finding you. Seeing the madness of Gertrude before she was Gertrude and choosing to adopt anyway. Listening to her desire for Alice."

"*C'est vraie.* However—"

"Ahhh, however…"

"Oui—even visible signs mean nothing unless you take the time to see through the surface."

Marie just nodded as she stroked Alice and scratched Gertrude's ear almost simultaneously. Then she fell deep into a thought.

"What?" I asked in an abrupt manner. It was my way to wake her and encourage her to talk.

"It's just…"

"Oh, come on, out with it."

"Her love for the young girl, her student—the one who loses her mother to cancer. Don't you ever wish we had a child?"

"No, never. I never wanted to be a mother and never wanted to have a child," I said vehemently.

"No, it's not that I wished to become a mother, like the character in the movie. But, don't you ever wish there were more young people, young energy in our life? Don't you ever wish we had someone to carry on our story, someone young enough to remember us?"

We both became quiet. We could not speak. We could not speak the unspeakable. The bus ride home was in total silence. I became lost in sadness.

"What?" punctured my ear and thoughts. It was uttered half-jokingly, an imitation of my strong Italian Philadelphia accent. Usually, I would laugh at Marie's bad imitation.

MICHELLE A. GABOW

However, life at this moment was not quirky or funny. The reverie it broke was not a pleasant one.

We descended the steps of the bus at our stop on rue Blanche.

"We should talk." My lips broke into an irrepressible quiver.

"Isn't that what we've been doing and do so well all the time?"

"You are being deliberately obtuse."

"Perhaps—"

"Perhaps shit!" I yelled. I couldn't believe I was screaming at Marie in public.

Marie just snickered and kept on walking.

"Don't walk away from me!" I screeched to her back.

She kept walking.

I was enraged.

"About the cancer. About dying," I cried out.

Marie executed a vehement about-face and declared, "No!"

"No?" I questioned, now much closer to her face, "Not now? Not later? Not ever?"

That's when it happened. Both Gertrude and Alice stopped midstream, literally, from a pee, and were equally focused across the street. They were both very still, at attention. At first, I thought that there were two other dogs across the street. But no. The street was *dogless*. Then, it was as if both Marie and I caught whatever they had. Our eyes were pulled like a magnet in the same direction.

Two women, one black, the other white, were sitting close together at our favorite outdoor café, Au P'tit Douai. There was a strange sensation in my body, prickly, alive, but unmovable, frozen. It's as if we pressed the pause button

GOD IS A DOG

on our own film. No, more than that. We were transfixed, locked into younger and older versions of ourselves. All six of us were time travelers. None of us could budge. What Gertrude and Alice saw, I do not know. For a split second—because that's all it was—I imagined that they were looking at versions of themselves also. As if they knew that a Yorkie and a Coton de Tulear were left at home, wherever *home* was for these two women.

They were not from here; that's for sure. I don't know, but I had a distinct impression that they, too, were from the United States. Were they the newest version of us? Lovers in Paris. Were they looking in a mirror, the opposite of Dorian Grey, and seeing who they could become? Like I said, in no more than a second, Gertrude was lifting her leg to pee (she did that). It was over.

We continued our walk to our door. But as I glanced back, I noticed the darker woman had grabbed the thigh of her partner, without the slightest fear or worry. I wondered if Marie had seen the same thing.

When we reached our blue door (even the doors in Paris are romantic), I noticed that Marie was fiddling with her keys more than usual. When I went to help her, she grabbed my head, looked me in the eye, bent my neck while pulling the back of my chignon, loosened my hair, curved her arm as to hold the small of my back, and gave me a kiss that made my blood rush. I melted in her strong arms like I did at nineteen, mesmerized by a passion I had never known before Marie. She held me like that, our lips parted, her tongue in my mouth. In public. Forever.

THE TRUTH ABOUT BARRY AND MARC

THE LINES FOR THE MANET exhibit twisted and turned for hours. In the Paris rain, we slithered like snakes to make our way inside L'Orsay. Although exhausted, we had little regret. However, our return trip on the 68 bus going in the wrong direction to the outskirts of Paris unhinged fits of hysterics. It was the *finale of lost.* After our wild bout, Michelle soberly pronounced, "Now, we really get to see my people and the Paris ghetto. We would have missed this truth."

We took another 68 bus at the end of the line home and bumped into a small aromatic bistro in "our" *neuvième.* After a huge glass of *vin rouge,* we were mutually humming.

Out our small window, an athletic, bald, middle-aged (whatever that is now) man was walking his bulldog. The dog's at one time thick and strong body was now too heavy for his legs—more like stubs—to carry. Yet, there was something regal and magnificent about him. I asked Michelle, who was closer to the camera and window, to get a shot.

Barry, my name for the old bulldog today, was a difficult shot. He was barely walking, so the pose was easy, but he was behind a gate in the street. Michelle said it was as if he was in jail. The man, Marc (for today), was out of the picture. He had one of those long leashes that you can release or retrieve by pushing a button. Simultaneously, we both watched Marc pull Barry hard, jerking him several times. Even though we could not hear them, we could feel Barry's moan through the cafe window. Barry pulled back on his short back legs that were barely legs at all and tried to lie down. Marc tugged harder. His impatience was palpable. Michelle and I suffered the choke.

Needless to say, we were witness to this over our entrees, which no longer appetized. Although the meal was probably superb, it did not sit well in my stomach. It took a long while for me to finally fall into a deep sleep.

***

The next morning, I vividly experienced my second dream of my father in ten years. I caressed his smooth and soft face, and he blushed while he spoke. *"When I see you, I'm aglow."* I was thrilled to see him too. He wasn't frail from the chemo, nor was he eighty years old—maybe fifty, if a day. Energetic, full of mischief, and very much alive. His hair was still black and wavy, and a Cole Porter tune was ready to burst from his lips. He had come because he wanted to visit my chiropractor. Something was wrong but it wasn't clear what it was. After his appointment, the chiropractor—who looked surprisingly like Dad—told me

MICHELLE A. GABOW

what a charming and sweet man he was. He said that he enjoyed seeing him. So did I.

***

I danced out the door that same morning for our croissants, enveloped and boosted by his visit. My dad was with me in Paris; how cool was that? On my short walk to the pâtisserie, as luck would have it, I practically bumped into Marc and Barry. Marc was screaming and probably cursing in French at Barry, while still dragging him along the rough cement like a lump. However, I was not going to let anyone, especially Marc, destroy my mood. I was determined to get in his way. I wanted to call him by his real name: *Asshole*. How dare he treat Barry like this? How would he like it if someone choked him on his goddamn morning walk? He glared at me. I glared at him. We were in an American Western, our guns almost drawn. I was tough today and besides I was a head taller than Marc. Then this weird thing happened. I spoke in perfect French.

"C'est très difficile de regarder quelqu'un que vous aimez faire vieux et fraile, n'est pas?" Translation: it is very difficult to see someone you love get old and frail.

Marc's thin upper lip quivered as his mouth parted to answer, *"Oui."*

And as he turned away, I heard him whisper under his breath, *"C'est vrai."*

***

Today, as I write my story, I turn sixty-three.

A QUESTION OF PURPOSE

"I SAW MY FIRST HOMELESS DOG in Paris!"

Ellen, my close friend and writing partner in Paris, was thrilled about the sighting, as if she, too, was writing *God Is A Dog*. I made her describe him to me on the spot.

"Well," she said, "he—I think it was a he—was a yellow-tan." She pointed to her suede jacket hanging on the dining room chair. "That exact color."

"Was he long- or short-haired?"

"Short-haired with a long snout. He had black around his mouth and nose."

"What size was he?"

"Um, medium-sized but with long, spindle-like legs—"

"Did he look lost?" I was a little obsessed with the concept of *lost* since living in Paris.

"No," she answered assertively.

MICHELLE A. GABOW

"Did he have any strong identifying features?"

Ellen thought for a few seconds, and then her green eyes lit up. "His tail! His tail was black and stood up straight, like an exclamation point."

So, I was predisposed to find Henri, the suede homeless dog. For two days, an entire weekend, I sat at Au P'tit Douai, our corner café, only to view an assortment of pigeons, motorbikes of all colors (even pink), a blonde Miami Vice Parisian man walking a black-and-white Boston terrier, and a fairly fantastic woman dressed in sheets and blankets with painted eyebrows walking a tannish-pink toy poodle. She, however, gave me a *grande* ear-to-ear smile.

Nevertheless, no Henri; however, he already had his name.

On Monday, I had my *café au lait* at Au P'tit Douai around five in the afternoon, my usual dinner hour. Everything had been turned around since we had arrived in Paris. All my usual habits and rituals were blown out of sight and mind. For example, I told everyone—and it was the truth—that I only wrote in the late mornings and I could only write alone. Now, I had been writing stories in bed as Michelle was sleeping at 2:00 in the morning, and it didn't matter who was around. When the urge took hold, I would write like a maniac. It didn't matter if it was in the middle of a dress shop or climbing up Montmartre; I had to stop myself from whatever I was doing and write. It really forced me to question my own stories of self.

I was missing Michelle, this late afternoon in Paris, who was visiting her brother in Amsterdam. I sat inside the café because it felt like rain, with the window wide open at my favorite blue Formica table, ready to do a little journaling about Chelle, when I spotted him. Henri was sitting in front

GOD IS A DOG

of the closed E. Gless Patisser directly across the street. It was Monday and we were both disappointed. Henri faced the *pâtisserie* frozen in a shattered expectancy; his black tail dragged across the ground.

I quickly pulled out my cell. "Ellen, are you writing?" I gave her no time to answer. "Come down now; I've spotted Henri."

"Henri?"

"The suede dog."

"I'll be right there."

Descending four flights of stairs in a few seconds, Ellen was at my table, staring at Henri.

"Oh, my God, what are the odds?"

Henri stood up, taking his disappointment regarding the lack of croissant crumbs with him.

"Let's follow."

And before Ellen could finish, "Are you cra—," we were on our way.

There was Henri, walking with intention and pride, down rue Blanche, his tail in perfect exclamation. There we were, tripping over our sandals and cowboy boots, slinking behind Paris doorframes—the Looney Tunes characters of Bugs Bunny and Elmer Fudd. We weren't "The Rabbit."

I know that this was not the way Ellen would have chosen to spend her sixtieth birthday. It really was a hilarious sight: two women in their sixties, sneaking around corners, playing detective, without the slightest notion what it was that needed detecting. But then again, that says volumes about Ellen and her mischievous twinkle, her openness to adventure, her way of just being in the world. Ellen would wake up with a song, in the sweetest voice, but her voice also had range. She could easily switch to deep, low, jazzy tones when necessary and vital to the song. She recognized that singing, like living, was not a luxury. So, as crazy as it seems, this was not out of character for either of us.

Henri made a quick left on rue Chaptal. Did he know we were hot on his trail? Was he trying to lose us? He stopped at the Musée De La Vie Romatinque, our favorite café, sniffed, and walked away. Although delicious, the food was not cooked or baked on the premises, so the aroma did not waft from the black iron gate. Henri continued, bearing *à droit* on rue La Bruyère. We passed the dazzling red Théâtre de la Bruyère, set back on our left. It was right around the corner from our apartment and yet somehow had eluded us.

Henri sauntered at a slower gate down a street, which led almost to Saint Georges métro. Ellen and I halted. Across the street was a simple but elegant church, standing by itself on its own street. It had an aura that illuminated the neighborhood surrounding it. We remained as still as the church, infused with its beauty.

Simultaneously, Ellen and I remembered Henri and like syncopated swimmers, turned our heads left. Henri lifted his snout, sniffed into the air and stood there for more than a few moments. Ellen and I gave each other a questioning glance. Was Henri actually waiting for us to catch up?

When we were closer, Henri crossed the street to an outdoor grocery. We followed. He waited patiently. For us? For the storekeeper? The fruits and veggies were outrageous—plump and colorful and delightful in every way to our touch, sight, and sense of smell. Ellen rapidly gathered a bunch of blackberries, figs, and peaches. Okay, this was absurd. Henri was actually waiting for us. The

GOD IS A DOG

storekeeper gave him pieces of cheese that Henri chewed slowly, a real connoisseur. They had some kind of language between them, a conversation of sorts. Ellen gathered more fruit and vegetables: vibrant red cherries, juicy tomatoes, and even a sliver of Brie cheese. Henri received leftover brie. Then it dawned on both of us. Damned if Henri wasn't being paid for his services.

We couldn't help but feel used. It took us a second to realize that we were famished and we decided to leave Henri to his own devices, which at this point were pretty attuned. Not quite a half block away was a small plaza with all these wonderful outdoor cafes. We chose the No Stress Café because of the name and sat at the table on the outer edge. Both of us ordered the same thing, *omelettes, pommes frites,* and *café crème.*

When we looked up from our menu, there was Henri, sitting at attention, facing us. Was he smiling? The man at the table next to us remarked, *"Qu'est-ce qu'un chien bien formés."* He repeated it in a thick French accent. "What a well-trained dog."

CHIEN, LE CHIEN

BY ADRIAN MOSKOWITZ

HAROLD SINGER WAS A MEAN son of a bitch. My mom told me never to say that out loud, even though she knew it was true. I think that makes me a liar, don't you? I'm not afraid to tell you right here and now: he was a mean son of a bitch and deserved to die a horrible, gruesome death.

The thing that makes me so pissed off about Lillian Moskowitz, my mom, is how she could come up with a million and one excuses for Mr. Singer, but not a one for my dad. "Mr. Singer has a hard life; his wife of thirty years passed away last year." "Mr. Singer has a problem with alcohol." That means he's a drunken bastard, and we should forgive him for that? But the one that gets me most of all is, "Mr. Singer really loves his dog; he just has a funny way of showing it." Bullshit! Pure bullshit!

GOD IS A DOG

He calls his dog Chien, which is *dog* in French. He doesn't even have a name. He locks him in a cage, sometimes in his own piss and shit. How can a person, a real person, do that, I ask you? And I know for an absolute, indisputable fact that the "poor" Mr. Singer beats Chien. I saw him through the window across the courtyard. We all live on the ground floor, which is Chien's, and my, saving grace.

On the other hand, my dad, Stephen Moskowitz, a good guy and great dad, did one stupid thing. Just one. They called him a "scam artist," which really doesn't mean *artist*. He sort of just took from one person to pay another. He never physically hurt anybody. Excuses up the wazoo for Mr. Singer. But my dad lands us on the other side of the world. I told Mom that when he comes for me—and he will come for me—I'm splitting this scene. And she could have her Paris and Mr. Singer.

I miss my dad. I don't belong here. Well, if I'm to be completely honest, which of course is who I am to my core, I didn't fit in in Philly either. I'm not like the other girls, never have been. Mom always said that I was my own person. I have to give her that. Dad suspected that she contributed to my lack of sixth-grade success. He accused her of "aiding and abetting." He bought me dresses, which somehow always mysteriously disappeared. He blamed it on Mom. She never said a word. But I knew that she knew that the holes I was digging in our backyard were for their burial. I even had little funerals for all the dead dresses. I began each funeral with the Jewish prayer: "*El maley rachamin shochen bam'romin hamtzey bam'romim hamtzey...*"

Aiding and *abetting* became my favorite *A* words. The beginning of the alphabet, the seed of something to come, the first taste of a banana split. As soon as I met Chien and discovered the real truth, I knew that our friendship, my only one in Paris, would be about my favorite *A* words.

Chien was a strange dog. We didn't know if Chien was a he or a she. Mom said that maybe she/he was a eunuch, which is neither man or woman or maybe both. I couldn't believe it; there was a word for Chien and me.

We loved each other at first sight.

***

Adrian Moskowitz never begged for anything in an entire lifetime. So when I got down on my knees and begged my mom to adopt Chien, she was a little in shock. Who could blame her? I mean, I was down on my hands and knees, for heaven's sake.

"Please—Chien is being neglected and hurt. Please, we need to adopt her!"

"We can't adopt him," was her response.

"Then we must steal him from the brutal Mr. Singer," I cried. "We have no choice. Can't you see? Do you ever look at Chien? She'll die, I tell you. She's dying!"

Mom held me in her arms. I didn't need to be held. I needed action. Again, why is it we could travel around half the world but somehow were unable to go across the courtyard and rescue Chien? Mom got it wrong yet again. I wasn't sad; I was livid.

The next day, Mom told me that she had a surprise. She was singing in the mirror, and to tell the truth, it was the first time I saw her smile since we left the States. I, too, couldn't contain my excitement. I knew she had talked to Mr. Singer and he said, "Yes, take the bastard." I could see his lips moving and hear him saying that clearly.

GOD IS A DOG

We walked down rue de Clichy a few blocks. I was a little confused but still elated. I began to skip. Now, Adrian Moskowitz doesn't skip. So that just shows you how elated I was. Then we turned into a small store called Chien et Chat Amour. There were a bunch of dogs, cats, birds, and turtles, all in cages similar to Chien's cage in Mr. Singer's jailhouse.

"Bonjour, Madame Moskowitz," said the zookeeper.

"Bonjour, Paul," replied my mom back.

Cute. Real cute, I thought. *Now, let's get out of here.*

Then Mrs. Moskowitz turns to me; her voice had a strange lilt. "Pick any dog you want, my darling."

"What?" I was unable to exclaim. Any dog? I didn't want any dog. Was she out of her damn mind? I wanted Chien! I loved Chien! Chien was supposed to be mine!

But I couldn't speak. All I could do was run as fast as my legs could take me. I jolted out of Animal Farm.

I ran better than ever before. My legs couldn't go fast enough. When I got to the neighborhood park, I just ran in circles, screaming like a madwoman. I was afraid. Could a person explode? I finally ran home to my bed and banged my door shut.

I wouldn't utter a word to Mrs. Moskowitz for weeks. Our apartment reverberated with the loudest silence in history. I wanted to punish her. I had planned to never speak to her or anyone again—that is, until my dad came to set Chien and me free. Until then, I would just wait in silence.

But I did notice things. I noticed that Mrs. Moskowitz's smile had completely disappeared. I noticed that her hair just didn't look right. She hadn't washed it in days, maybe weeks. One morning, I saw her on the toilet, her head

MICHELLE A. GABOW

tucked between her knees, sobbing. I felt my heart tear open.

She was as lonely, as sad, as broken as Chien.

The next morning, before my last day of silent summer school, I made her a pot of strong coffee, kissed her on the forehead, and revised my plans.

***

I was determined to spend quality time with Chien every day—no matter what. So, I began to study Mr. Singer's habits and recorded everything—I mean *everything*—in my *petit* notebook. I was more Nancy Drew than Nancy Drew. Dad used to read me those stories each night before bed. Or was it Mom? My favorite was *Nancy Drew and the Brass Bound Trunk*. I couldn't understand that if we were going to travel to Europe, why we couldn't go on an ocean liner. That, at least, was an adventure. But by airplane? Echhh. One day we lived in Philly as a family, the next in Paris, in separate worlds, with an ocean between us. It really wasn't fair.

Mom said, too often for my taste, that life wasn't fair. I was hell-bent on evening out the odds.

The first page of my notebook looked like this:

7:00 a.m. -Harold Singer lets Chien into courtyard.
7:10 a.m. -Calls Chien to come in the house.

*Not much time to take a piss or shit, let alone walk... small dogs, like small people, need a lot of exercise. I should know.

GOD IS A DOG

7:30–11:15 a.m.	-Harold Singer leaves his filthy apartment for the day.
11:15a.m.–12:45 p.m.	-Comes home. Drinks 2 beers, today eats some salami right off the roll. Echhh!
	-Does not let Chien out of cage.
	-Falls asleep on ratty chair.

Check out how sound he sleeps—easy to climb in window from courtyard.

7:00 p.m.	-Harold Singer wakes up.
	-Forgets to feed Chien.
	-Lets Chien out. After 2 minutes, calls him back.
	-Chien doesn't return right away. When she does, Singer beats her and locks her in cage.
11:00 p.m.	-Returns home. Lets Chien out. Sleeps on ratty chair.

I had been investigating Harold Singer for several weeks. His routine was rarely altered but for two exceptions. Sometimes he would beat Chien and sometimes not. Sometimes he would remember to feed him. The only new info in my investigation was that Mom said that she thought he was retired. He was tired, all right. I discovered, to my total delight, that nothing—and I mean *nothing*—could or would wake the dead Mr. Singer. I tried clashing pans, a flashlight in his closed eyes, singing loudly, feathers up his nose. His deafening snore might abate for a second

MICHELLE A. GABOW

but would return soon after to shake this whole goddamn apartment.

So there was plenty of time for Chien and I to have a real friendship. We'd go on morning walks around the park. He was full of surprises. Dad—or was it Mom?—once said that another name for God is Surprise. He would travel on paths around our neighborhood that I never knew existed. We became friendly with many new storeowners. Our friendship seemed to make adults smile. Through Chien, I was learning about many new places and out-of-the-way streets. Paris was beginning to be fun. A real adventure every day.

I had told Mom that I was given Mr. Singer's permission. For some reason, she never questioned me further. I think she, too, was happy that I had a real friend in Paris. Each day, I cleaned Chien's cage, fed her, gave her water, and loved her. The cage was large, and occasionally I would crawl in with him and cuddle. I realized that I envied Chien a bit; he could leave his cage. Mine might be invisible to the world but was very much a cage—a bona fide prison, in fact. There were times—and I don't mind saying so—that I had very angry conversations with God. Sometimes, instead of praying, I would curse him. If he really existed and was soooo omnipotent, why would he put me in a girl's body? Why would he move me away from my father? How could he let Mr. Singer live and be so cruel and nasty to Chien? Dad always said I had too many questions for a girl. Maybe.

***

Epiphany is a sudden realization or an appearance of God. I know this now because I asked Mom about having truth hit you so hard over the head, like a ton of bricks,

GOD IS A DOG

that it made you realize nothing would ever be the same again. I spared her the details. She just smiled, and I swear I heard a little chuckle. "You had an epiphany," she said. So I looked it up.

I knew I was on the right track when three questions popped into my brain. They were: Do I need to rethink God? Did Mom have an epiphany? And will I have to change my entire life now that I am finally happy?

So I know you're wondering, because I would be too, how an epiphany happens. The thing is, I don't know if it's so sudden, like the dictionary says. It *kinda* creeps up on you and one day it just so "is" that you can't avoid it. That's the way it was with Chien and me.

We were going on our merry—or maybe not-so-merry— way for weeks, until that Thursday morning on August 8. It was a morning like any other morning. Mr. Harold "son of a bitch" Singer was off to his retirement, and I was picking up Chien for our morning walk. I had loads of energy because I was excited about what path Chien would take me on that day. As I said, every day was an adventure with Chien. I don't know how he knew the streets so well. After all, he had been locked in a cage since we met. He seemed to have a sixth sense, and I totally trusted and enjoyed our trips through Paris.

On that Thursday morning, the apartment seemed sad. Can a room really take the shape of a feeling? I opened the cage, but Chien didn't move. When I tried to coax him, he began to whimper, and I noticed blood on his leg, what seemed like a bruise around his lip, and that his right eye barely opened. I wiped up the blood and crawled in the cage with him and cried my heart out. We left the cage together and went on what I thought was to be a short walk.

47

MICHELLE A. GABOW

We must have been quite the sight. Chien was limping and whimpering; I was hysterical crying, sometimes using my full lungs.

When I returned home, Mom asked me if I was okay. I knew my eyes were bloodshot and my face had that blotchy look I so hated, so I ran to my room and shut the door. My mom opened the door and came in. I screamed at her, "Get out. I hate you! Leave me alone. Didn't you see that my door was closed? *Get out now!*"

She didn't listen; she sat on my bed and held me tighter than ever before. I began to bawl like a freakin' baby. I couldn't stop the tears. Sometimes I'm so damn girly. She rocked me in her arms. "It's going to be all right. It's all right," she repeated several times. For the first time in a long while, I knew that she was right.

The next morning was very odd. First of all, it was afternoon, and I awoke to the smell of freshly baked chocolate chip cookies. The apartment seemed light and happy. A room *can* really take the shape of a feeling. I went in for breakfast and asked, rightly so, "What's up?"

"Nothing. Everything. Nothing," Mom answered— almost sang.

Okay. What was that supposed to mean? She was being even more mysterious than I had ever been.

When I sat down to eat my breakfast cereal, I found chocolate ice cream. Chocolate ice cream for breakfast? I thought, *Damn, I really sent Mom over the edge.* She poured a cup of coffee for herself and then me. I mean, I'm only twelve. A cup of coffee?

After that, she said, and I swear this is true, "Eat your ice cream before it melts," and placed a freshly baked cookie on my plate.

GOD IS A DOG

I began to eat when she whispered, almost out of the blue, "Mrs. Kramer came over today."

Like I care. Mom likes her because she speaks English. I think that she has a big mouth and can't keep anything to herself. I feigned interest. Really, I just didn't know how to react.

"She let me know that Chien is missing."

I could barely swallow my ice cream.

"She thinks perhaps he ran away."

I tried to keep a poker face.

"I told her that you would be heartbroken."

I almost choked but regained my composure.

"But you know what I think…" she teased.

Okay, she was taunting me now.

"Do you?" she repeated differently.

"No," I answered.

Then everything went quiet for hours, well, maybe just a few minutes. I began to think of Chien. Running around the park, having a new adventure on the Paris streets, meeting a really wonderful person who gave him shelter. But most of all, I imagined that if Chien could escape a cage, maybe with a little help, I could too.

My mother's words broke my little reverie. "I think that…" Long pause…

It became crystal clear to me that my brand of drama was not uncommon in my family.

"Chien had herself an epiphany," she finally announced.

Mrs. Moskowitz, my mom, cradled her large French coffee cup in both hands and lifted it to her lips, almost but not quite concealing a grin.

49

ISABELLA ET KARIN, A LOVE STORY

BY ISABELLA LOVE

"ISABELLA... ISABELLA..." I LOVED THE way Karin sang my name each morning. Although she always overslept—when I had been up for more than an hour—she was easy to forgive. So easy. Yes, of course it was love. I won't bore you with the details of how we met or even why the attraction was so bizarrely strong. We met and it was love at first sight. *C'est tout.*

I'm sure you're wondering why my English is so *parfait.* Well, it wasn't easy, this language, but it is Karin's native language. Although she has lived in Paris for more than thirty years, English is still spoken in our home. I feel sexy and alive in French, but somehow more honest in English.

One of the many reasons I stayed in love with Karin is because we both shared an appreciation for ritual. Each morning, we would have our coffee at Le Bar de Relais, where we were well known by Jean, the waiter and proprietor. As soon as we would sit, our espresso and *croissant avec beurre* would be placed at our regular table, no questions asked. That's the other thing: we weren't afraid of silence, Karin and I. We relished it as we sat and watched all the sad working people on their morning trips. Neither of us really worked. Well, I was living on her largesse, and she was still writing her column for *The Post*. She was also writing a novel, *Theory of Least Regret*. An exorbitant advance had been sent, and as Karin told me quite firmly, every day, it was almost *une fait complète*.

I suppose if one had been looking at Karin from a strictly objective perspective, she was not beautiful. She was beautifully round though. Okay, objective: she was round and rather wrinkled for her sixty-three years. I told her time and time again, it was from too much smoking. She would just say, *"C'est très sexy quand je fume. Non?"* *C'est vrai.* It was. Her hair was her freedom flag. It was double salt to pepper, medium length, very curly, and never combed. Her clothes were mismatched, always dark, and had a kind of elegant, funky, sixties cool to them. But her shoes were the *piece de resistance.*

There was always a passerby who would stop her in the street to remark about them. Jean was her biggest fan. This morning, he simply oozed about her shoes. I had a certain pride because I had accompanied Karin on that particular shopping trip to her favorite store, Baabou Paris, in the *neuvième* about a month ago. It was located straight down rue Douai, right on rue des Martyrs, and boasted as *"La Mode put Toutes les Filles,"* and it was. Large sizes and styles galore for every woman. We felt comfortable in that small store, so it was normal to dish out a whole paycheck for her Trippen shoes from Berlin. They were incredible black, thick, laced-up sandals with two raised sections at the foot, one on the ball of her foot and one on her heel. They were a magnificent sculpture that made her look strikingly taller and were her prized possession as of late.

"So," Karin told Kika, our saleswoman and friend, "lunches were out of the question for a month and it's worth every bite of Jean's quiche." When Karin wore them, we both recognized that this was going to be a good writing day.

Although they were fun and cute, I was always a little concerned when she wore her red, laced-up Keds, just for the fact that it meant more walking and less writing. Don't get me wrong, I love to walk. We have that in common, but since retirement, my arthritis has set in, and I do need more rest than I ever imagined.

I think that many friends were surprised that we'd been together for so long. I was quite a looker in my day and very popular with the ladies. I was a well-established model known for my stature, thick, long, blue-black mane cascading down my back (which, by the way, has remained true to color without a touch of dye to this day), and perfect proportions. But then again, Karin was the more interesting and exciting of the two of us.

She had a *joie de vivre* that couldn't be matched, a sense of the absurd and theatrical, and the most amazing theories about love, loss, and life. Okay, she was a little moody. But, hey, that's to be expected. It comes with certain brilliance. And it was amazing what a few morning kisses could accomplish. I knew I was her anchor. Yet, it was the two of us together that made each of us. We knew that truth deep in our souls.

GOD IS A DOG

Am I making it sound like we had the perfect relationship? Or that we never fought? If so, that would be a lie. Believe me, if I were telling you this in French, although we were brooding at times, I would skip the clashes. And there were plenty. Suffice it to say, our natures were very different. *Ahhhh*, you're thinking. *Vive la différence!* Of course, that was part of the attraction. But for the daily life of a relationship, it was *très difficile.*

First of all, I was so much more close to the earth than she was. Her head was truly in the clouds. There were times she would have literally stepped into traffic if it weren't for me. And I don't mind telling you, that's a hell of a lot of responsibility.

For me, life was all about the moment; not that I was a Buddhist or anything—it was just my nature. She was always perseverating about the past or fixated on the future. I swear, the only time she was in the present on her own and focused for a period of time was when she was writing. It was important to keep her writing and on track. Another responsibility. So, enjoying our coffee and people-watching was wonderful, but equally as good was getting Karin back to the apartment and writing. Truth be told, I could have sat at the café for the entire day. However, on this particular day, right in the middle of a delicious bite, I could detect something happening. Karin's eyes began clouding up and an incessant sniffling erupted.

I didn't want to be. Truly I didn't. But I found myself extremely annoyed. Here we were at our favorite café, on a perfect day in Paris—70 degrees, sunny, with a light, but sweet wind—she in her fantastic shoes, me looking absolutely exquisite for my age, and both of us eating the best croissants on Montmartre, and damned if she wasn't crying. Again.

MICHELLE A. GABOW

I tried to be compassionate and gave her my understanding eyes, but I really didn't feel it.

"In a week, it will be ten years, Isabella. Ten years."

I nodded sympathetically but thought, *Oh, God, we're on this again.*

"She was such a character, wasn't she?"

I was quiet. Really, there was no need to answer.

"Remember our last trip to Boston, when she was still well enough to talk? There she was, sitting in the middle of the dementia ward on that fourth floor at Hebrew Rehab, her legs folded like a queen. When the doctor came to question her, she stared right through him and said, 'Fuck you.' He couldn't believe his ears. He had to look again. Then she mouthed, 'Fuck' and pointed to him, '... you.' We all had a good laugh in her room."

She smiled, and I gave her the best smile I could.

"You know I thought that she never approved of our relationship. But she truly got to see you and love you."

I didn't really remember that.

"Her favorite line was, 'I hate old people.' I wish for just one day, we could have flown her here, wheeled her into the café, and all of us could have had croissants and appreciated people of all ages and sizes walking by. She would have loved that."

I love it now, I thought but did not utter. Karin often insisted that I was unable to support her when she was sad and accused me of barking at her. This was challenging for me, but I stifled my bark superbly. I was quite proud of myself.

Who says that you can't teach an old dog new tricks?

We left—and walked home on opposite sides of the street. We weren't fighting but we needed our separate

GOD IS A DOG

spaces today. I loved all the sounds and sights of Paris, to look in all the store windows and to feel the wind in my hair. She needed to be one with her thoughts and memories.

When we arrived at our small, but bright, fifth-floor rented flat, we were both extremely fatigued. I had to lie down immediately. Karin was doing something in the kitchen. When I looked up, she appeared with a special bacon treat she had prepared for me. She gently placed it next to me in bed and stroked my belly. The last thing I remember, before I fell into a deep sleep, was the sound of computer keys as our two vastly unique worlds converged and dared me to dream.

COUP DE FOUDRE

FOUND PARIS. OR MAYBE PARIS found me, with a longing so vast that it couldn't possibly belong to my own self. Grieving does that. A tornado whirls through, casts you out the door into the wind, with no direction, no map, and most definitely no GPS.

Paris—what gust pushed me here with complete certainty and without tangible reason? The city had nothing to do with my plays, my sabbatical project, or my current life. Yet, there really is an answer to that question. A perfectly ridiculous, and even foolish, answer, but one that bursts with infinite seduction, promise, and possibilities.

I flew here... *to get lost...* again... and again... and again. How can one help it in this city of never-ending circles? Spiraling mazes. At first, being part of this experiment was no fun. I didn't like being my own guinea pig.

In the beginning… sounds like the Bible. My own Bible, that is. It was the cause of constant friction between Chelle, my partner of thirty years, and me.

"No, I'm sure it's this way," I urged.

"Are you—really? Because, according to my calculations, Monmartre goes up, not down,"

"How about the name of a street. That would be helpful."

"Well, damn, the street names keep changing," alleged Chelle.

"So do your moods."

"What was that?"

Silence.

"Anyway, I can't learn directions by names of streets. I have a visual memory," Chelle stipulated.

"Guess what?"

"What?"

"Visually, we're fucked."

We had a hundred different versions of that conversation in the first week. But… The *but* really does stand on her own. It became the surprises we found in the middle of being lost—sometimes in the middle of a grand-mal argument or one of our many silent battles—that could turn those ordinary, often tense moments into magic.

Ibrahim

Going up hill. What are we searching for? Up the backside of Sacré-Cœur. Michelle is suspended in front of a café; she takes a whiff and smiles. "That's food!" What a nose. I am clueless. Inside, everything is lavender, flowers, and views of rooftops and Paris. Are we dreaming? Our waiter

MICHELLE A. GABOW

invites us in, while kissing us on each cheek. Do we know him? His name is Ibrahim. We do not yet know that he is a human treasure. His brother owns the restaurant. He is a dentist in Egypt. He loves that we are theater artists. He brings out poetry books, early editions of Proust, Faustus, Genet, reads out loud, shows us poems from friends he keeps in a book behind the counter. Tells us that all his books cost no more than a dollar in a flea market in Paris. Calls Michelle his sister. Asks me to write him something for his book. I write, "To Ibrahim, the poet of heart." We talk about his theater friends who come in late at night and stay until the morning; he wants us to meet them. We talk of art and poetic lives, his sister who is ill in the States, and our dreams, all while we drink red wine and mint tea. "Michelle," he laughs, "my sister. " The café is ours. There is no one else in it this hot afternoon until evening. Are we in a movie? As we leave, Ibrahim kisses us full of tears. The cook, Ibrahim's brother (the owner), and his wife come out and kiss each cheek. How long have we actually known each other? We lose our sense—of time.

Dream of a Butterfly

Home is this way? No, no, no. That…

Bewildered and now just a little drunk, we bump into a small park, which is covered with posters.

> Rêve du Papillion
> Le 4 et 5 juin 2011 a 19h30
> Aux Arènes de Montmartre
> 5 E

We are Alice from Wonderland, except for the fact that we pay five euros. Voila! Natural cement benches, full of children, elders, Parisians, and a scattering of tourists. We circle the stage. Chaotic, physical metaphors rise like balloons and pop. Transformation is the language, so language is no longer a barrier. As the actors play, the walls come down. Unlike anything in Boston. We are reminded why we do theater. We are asked questions: *Qui-suis je?* (Who am I?); *Qu'est-ce que j'ai perdu?* (What did I lose?); and *Ai-je vraiment perdu quelque chose?* (Did I really lose something?). Over and over, like kōans or mantras. When the play ends, everyone, actors and audience, dance on stage. Michelle and I continue the dance home, not like women in our fifties and sixties, but like our own children, if we had any.

Lucienne *et* Hank

Friends of friends of friends. Ellen, my writing partner, was determined to take them out to dinner, a thank you for finding our apartment. I was determined to stay home. Until, that is, I met Lucienne—so full of grace, energy, and stories. She knew Leontyne Price and Jean Seberg in her youth, traveled to Africa, married at forty-five, to Hank (a nice Jewish boy fourteen years her junior). Now Lucienne, an Afro-Cuban eighty-five-year-old woman, dances Zumba three times a week and remains close to her nine children that she and Hank adopted "from the heart." Hank, a writer, is truly inquisitive about us and passionate, a rare breed of man. After a dinner of wild conversation and much laughter (Lucienne can drink us all under the table),

MICHELLE A. GABOW

Hank leaves early to accept a New York business call. Ellen and I walk home with Lucienne. I have trouble keeping up. Lucienne grabs my hand in hers, and we walk close and tight in our stories.

"Are we lost?" asks Lucienne.

"No," says Ellen assuredly.

"When Hank asks me to turn right, I turn left—"

"Always a good turn," I kid.

"Absolutely," Lucienne laughs in cahoots, as if we're playing a game that only the three of us know. A secret we are keeping together. "Don't know my left from my right. Always been this way. My whole life, I'm getting lost."

"We underestimate lost," I say, drawing from my newfound knowledge.

"Yes!" she agrees excitedly, as if winning the lottery. "Yes, yes." She giggles like a child but not childishly. "Always felt a little sorry for those with a strong direction."

Lucienne makes a strange face by twisting her mouth to the left, keeping it open and round, and then clasps my wrist and guides my hand to her heart, a heart that has no difficulty speaking. "They miss moments... like this."

Isabelle

Ellen rushes up four flights of stairs and into the apartment, out of breath but not out of energy. She has been on an adventure of lost and found.

"I've just been to the most fabulous shop. Clothes that make your mouth water. All sizes. Shoes you only dream of."

I don't really dream of shoes.

"You have to come back with me and meet Isabelle."

GOD IS A DOG

"Isabelle?"

"Tomorrow."

"I have to—"

"Of course, after we work."

I'm increasingly realizing that this whole "yes" thing is a difficult task for me. But Ellen is unstoppable, and before you know it, I'm in the middle of a new story and Ellen is trying on shoes. She is in deliberation for what seems like hours. Decision-making is not her forte. However, as far as Lucienne and Isabelle, it was impeccable. Maybe it's just shoes. Instead of impatience or pressure to sell, Isabelle, the Parisian saleswoman, is charmed. She pulls clothes and shoes from the shelves and hangers like a ballet dancer. The cast of sales characters joins her in the ultimate dance ensemble.

Like an old penny, Ellen and I keep reappearing on her doorstep. "*Enchanté*," she greets each time, with a vigorous certainty and French kisses. We can never get enough enchantment. My mother would always ask me, "Who does she look like that we know?" The answer, Mom, is: a forty-five-year-old alignment of Audrey Hepburn and Juliette Binoche. With black-framed glasses they never wore in public. Without a doubt and without makeup.

On one visit, she turns up the music and announces in her French/English, "This is my favorite song." It's Lou Reed singing, "Walk on the Wild Side." Come on—Lou Reed?

Doo do doo do doo do do doo... Isabelle decides that we *must* have wine together ... doo do doo do do... We're out the door. Doo do doo do doo do do doo, doo do doo do doo do do doo... We're eating and drinking at a café with a waiter named Toni (I could never say it like she does) for four hours.

61

MICHELLE A. GABOW

"Oh, my grandma," Isabelle sighs. We are somewhere in the middle of a conversation and our lives. "When I would go to visit her, she was always upset about something my grandpa was doing. Finally, I told her that he died a few years ago. And she said, 'Oh, why didn't you tell me?'"

"When my mom asked me over and over to call Dad on the phone," I chimed in; I told her, "Mom, I can't do that because I believe he's six feet under. She replied rather matter-of-factly, 'And I don't.'"

Isabelle said, "That was that. Two different realities. Who's to say?"

"One day, I walked in on my father in the home," Ellen interjected. "I witnessed him having a conversation in someone else's room. He was talking and talking. The man in bed kept screaming, 'Get out,' but my father continued as if they were having a perfectly normal conversation. The man kept screaming, 'Get out!' And when my dad left, he waved good-bye and said, 'Nice talking to you.'"

We all just smiled. We knew these stories so well. Somehow the humor and camaraderie make them hurt just a little less. This night while talking of divorce, break-ups and change, Isabelle says out of nowhere, "You will be published." I start to object and she repeats, "No, no, no, Michelle, you will be published," with a certainty that astounds me. Ellen nods her head.

The conversation changes, as quickly as a snap of a finger, to depression, which we all suffer from. All three of us consider ourselves depressives. This becomes the perfect opportunity for my parking-attendant story.

"One afternoon, at a small shopping mall, while leaving the lot, the parking attendant begins to laugh at me. I mean, real laughter. I check my nose for snot, my shirt for

GOD IS A DOG

a huge stain, and finally, she says, 'So good to see a happy person, singing, leaving the lot.' I had to reevaluate."

Ellen talks about the light and energy she feels in Isabelle, herself, and me. A similar spirit. Isabelle calls what we have *coup de foudre,* a love so strong that it's like lightning striking. "It's funny," Isabelle adds, "I always saw myself as a *lost soul.*"

What is this?

I nod so vehemently, I hurt my neck. Ellen nods in unison.

Suddenly, everybody in the café is quiet, their eyes glued to the man across the street. A middle-aged man with exceptionally long hair, carrying a pizza box, is singing. He is singing opera at the top of his lungs, with a glorious voice that bounces off the Paris building walls and gives this moment drama, awe, and the kind of heart that brings tears into being. Ellen leans against my shoulder and points. In front of our opera star, leading him, is a brown-suede dog with a black tail functioning as a baton. Or possibly an exclamation point!

Ellen lifts her glass. "What are the odds?"

ZERO

BY NATALIE TERRANOVA

The bedroom took the shape of Marie's lips,

open
in a perfect "**O**"

Our still hearts beat
the intolerable
mystery of life,

Circle.

the
mourning

Empty

kiss of a
liberated

One

spirit,

the merciless touch of void.

BEHIND THE VELVET CURTAIN

I'M SURE THAT WE HAVE some sort of courtyard to our apartment in the *neuvième*. It's simply invisible to the naked eye from our window. Our only view is of the windows in the building facing us, so close we can almost reach right in. In case these stories do get published, I want to personally thank the nameless woman who has the window box full of lush red roses that seem to become more beautiful with each passing day—and they are passing way too fast. This apartment atmosphere usually creates a fairly quiet setting for writing. But it's also pretty damn intimate.

I'm surrounded by the scents of great cooking when I'm starving, the sound of a dog somewhere below lapping water, a fight in the middle of the night—how dare he come an hour late to meet her friends, and then make-up sex, and make-up sex, and... They are extended family,

MICHELLE A. GABOW

even though I can only make out a word here and there, which in some cases is obviously not necessary.

Then there is the apartment with the deep-purple curtains, usually pulled but occasionally... Well, on occasion, the woman pulls the velvet theater curtain of her life and weeps—more like wails—into her empty window box. It's very jarring and terribly sad. On the day that Ellen and I pulled our sheer curtain and opened the window, we saw another woman stroking her hair, the crying lady's face deep in the box. For one second, the woman looked up from her box and we all faced each other. We were four women who all knew real heartbreak.

Both Ellen and I thought someone, someone close, had died. It touched our own recent grief. I found myself one night sobbing in my bed. *Grief is like that*, I thought. *Never-ending*. I wondered, *How do people carry all this loss and grief into old age?*

How?

When Ellen left to return to California, I was lonely. Sometimes, I remained awake all night, breathing in and out the vastness of space. I thought often of the woman behind the purple velvet curtain, alone. Could I really breathe without Michelle? I remember my mom saying after my dad's death, "Now, I'm only half a person." I got so angry. "What do you mean? You're a whole person." I can't even use youth as an excuse for my ignorance. I was fifty and still *très stupide*.

***

It's a girl! I wrapped her in a thick but scratchy blanket, not unlike the one that was covering me in my Parisian bed. The baby had the bluest eyes and strands of feathery,

GOD IS A DOG

blue-black hair. If fact, she was the spitting image of my mother, Tibie. As I held her, she began to laugh. I asked why such laughter, and she answered quite clearly. "The apartment is so vast." I wanted to tell someone that she spoke in a perfect sentence, but I knew no one would believe me.

I woke up to some woman screaming in orgasm. And I mean screaming. It did not have the same playfulness and pleasure as the young English woman and her French never-on-time boyfriend downstairs. But it did exceed in sheer volume. It was deafening. It would rise and fall to silence, rise and silence, all night long. I mean, how many *real* orgasms can one have? Now, I'm a pretty open gal to S&M sex, but this somehow didn't feel quite consensual. It was eerie and edgy and the passion felt more like actual one-sided pain. It stung me awake.

I yelled at Ellen across the living room, "Do you hear that?" and waited for an answer until I realized that she left three days ago. I was alone in the apartment. My only company was someone else's misery. I slinked over to the window, you know, the one that was practically inside the facing windows. I surveyed the entire building until the sound began to swell in my soul, and—you guessed it—directly behind the purple curtain. The thick, plush curtain could not hide the horror behind it.

That afternoon, a friend of Ellen's came by to return a pot she had borrowed from our apartment. She was a thirty-something New York lesbian with one of those bowl haircuts, adorned in a long, funky scarf with the reddest lipstick ever. I liked this new lesbian; she reminded me of myself at that age, only more sure of herself. I told her the story and talked about contacting the police. However, I

MICHELLE A. GABOW

wasn't completely sure what I was calling about. Was this about abuse? Could it be consensual? The young woman across from me on the red chair with redder lipstick related a recent story involving two of her friends: they were a little tipsy, so they were hailing a cab. A car with a group of men inside pulled up and asked them how much they were charging for the night. They kept trying to explain over and over that they were not prostitutes and were hailing a cab. The men got out of the car and proceeded to beat the two women. After a few bloody moments, people ran to their rescue, and the boys hopped back into their car. When the women reported it to the police, they actually snickered and hinted that perhaps one of the young women had drunk too much.

The IMF Chief, Dominique Strauss-Kahn, was only the tip of the iceberg.

The sex persisted for four long, miserable nights. Then, one day, it stopped. Just like that. I was relieved—, not that I'm trying to get myself off the hook. There are some hooks we should never be lifted from. I knew in my heart there were only two scenarios at this point, and they both sucked. Either she kicked the bastard out (which doesn't mean that he wouldn't come back) or she was dead.

One evening, through a sliver of curtain, I saw a woman getting dressed for a night on the town. I watched for more than a few moments as she covered her bruised arms and neck with powder and then dressed in her evening clothes. She was alive. Yet, I found myself grieving for her. Or maybe I was grieving my inability to act, my own fear that kept me frozen. Grief has many faces. Each time that we are unable to speak our truths because of our jobs, or fear of broken hearts, or money, or loss of respect, or our idyllic view about the way things should be, or simply because we won't be believed, we lay ourselves open to a different species of grief. Just as sad, but more haunting.

***

I'm sure you're wondering, *Where is the dog in this story?* After all, this book is titled *God Is a Dog.* And believe me, I tried to imagine one. At one point, I thought, *maybe there is a sad dog in the window and we lock into each other, helpless.* But the sap was just too damn thick. I had to come to the unfortunate conclusion that there was no dog behind that velvet curtain.

THE HUMAN HEART

BY NATALIE TERRANOVA

UDDENLY, THERE ARE BIRDS EVERYWHERE. At least ten sparrows are on the back and seat of my bench. Some are walking dangerously near my toes; one is entirely too close to my croissant. An unearthly, huge dove flaps her wings, flies to a tree, and looks at us ominously from the branch above. A lone crow munches on crumbs and stops to stare from the corner of his left eye for a good minute. Two ducks, out of nowhere, pause to discuss life as they pass. Where did they all come from? Pain attracts the wildest creatures.

We come here every day. The same park. The same tasteless croissant. The same bench. But this is the first time for all these birds. It feels like that old Hitchcock movie, but without the fear—or hope. I suppose Hitchcock wouldn't be Hitchcock without those primary emotions.

GOD IS A DOG

A woman with a baby carriage brings her infant to the old, kind woman with two cute dogs. The smaller dog snaps. I stick out my tongue. The mother leaves, outraged, cursing in French, not-so-under her breath. The other dog licks invisible tears from a familiar face.

"Life isn't fair," I say in my mind, but surprisingly, it bursts out of my mouth, loudly—very loudly and clear as a bell.

A young, dirty boy that I hadn't noticed sitting next to me says in perfect English with a familiar accent, "Sometimes."

For one moment, I am transported to Gimbels Department Store in Philadelphia and Marie. It was the *oi* sound in *times*. I quickly tear myself away from memory, regain my composure and tell him quite firmly to go away.

The little urchin doesn't move.

"Get the hell out of here!" the little old woman—me—screams. The entire park, all the mothers, a petite girl perched on top of a sliding board, several children throwing balls, and the scattering of bums here and there, are riveted for a second. It's a very small family park.

Unexpectedly, my tiny dog begins to run around the park in circles like a madwoman. I'm flabbergasted. Her canine partner walks to the middle, turns, and stares, following her friend with her eyes. She, too, appears confused.

"Gertrude," I call, "come. Now."

The boy on the bench looks up at me, tears in his eyes, and questions, in a voice like a girl, "He has a name?"

"Well, of course she has a name," I reply.

When Gertrude returns, she allows the boy to scratch her ear. I could swear my fat little Gertrude was purring, which is a completely new and unusual response for her

MICHELLE A. GABOW

in regards to a complete stranger. In fact, she only reacts that way with my Marie and on occasion with me. Then the boy—or was it a girl?—begins to weep. And I mean *weep*, in that disgusting way children can: eyes flooding, snot dripping into his mouth, face blotchy, pink, puffy, thick eyelids, sleeves soaking wet from wiping his runny nose. He can't stop. I refuse to comfort him. No, I don't refuse. I am unable.

The park mothers look worried. There is an odd but obvious buzzing throughout.

"Fuck you!" I yell with lungs that are new to me.

Their mouths open in one massive, horrified gape.

Laughter erupts from my bench mate. That's it, right from sobbing profusely to hysterical laughter—no control, whatsoever. Just as quickly, he exits his own laughter, opens his arms, and touches his chest. Obeying his instructions, Gertrude jumps in the urchin's lap. Alice and I are unable to move. We are dumbfounded. Our Gertrude usually has a visceral, and I might add, vicious reaction to the male species. She flares her little nostrils, lifts her upper lip above her teeth, and is in attack mode if any man comes within petting distance. I am actually doing a great imitation of her today. Marie would be proud.

It was Marie who first noticed her running madly in circles in the park, this park. We sat and watched from a bench, this bench. As she slowly inched closer and closer to our bench and croissant crumbs, we noticed dried blood around her left ear and mouth. Marie and I didn't have to speak. We all knew. She was ours; we were hers. Without even a word or a bark, she followed us home.

Alice nudges me out of my reverie as if to ask, *"Will you look at this?"* Gertrude is licking and dare I say, kissing, the

God Is a Dog

dirty boy's cheeks, nose, and ears before she decides to jump off the bench.

As we stand to leave, the pint-sized brat has the nerve—and at this point, it does take nerve—to grab my wrist with a hold that surprises me.

"Will I see the three of you again?" I could say that he was begging, but he wasn't. This foolish child appeared strangely sure of himself.

To my complete astonishment, a word flew out of my mouth. Truly, it escaped from what felt like a foreign country—or at the very least, someone else's lips. Yet, it was there, very present, in that moment, just the same.

"Yes," I answered.

THE PINK LADY SPEAKS ENGLISH

Miss Almira Gulch rides her bicycle madly into the sky during a tornado that brings Dorothy to Oz. She is determined to put a stop to Toto, who has been in her garden; that is, until she becomes the Wicked Witch of the West.

The pink lady has Almira's force and speed as she rides up Rue Blanche to the Moulin Rouge. I can almost hear the ominous music from *The Wizard*. However, she isn't on her way to becoming the Wicked Witch; or at least, not wicked.

I spot her the first time while having a morning croissant at my favorite café, which happens to be across the street from me. She is riding her pink bicycle while wearing a pale-pink wool cape, gray, sparkly stockings, and two-tone high heels; her very blonde hair is tied with pink ribbons, her age unknown. She cuts a stunning visage of beauty and freedom.

GOD IS A DOG

Two days later, I watch as she effortlessly hightails it uphill on her same pink bike in her pink wool cape and heels. The only problem is that today it is 90 degrees in Paris.

One day later, I have another pink lady sighting, in a different section in the *neuvième*. She has on her same clothes, no worse for wear. As I move closer, I notice that she is much older than I originally suspected, but how much older is unclear. She is meticulously tying her bicycle to a pole with a pink ribbon. I watch as she enters a health clinic across the street.

The last two sightings are the most dramatic. The first of these takes place near Le Louvre. Lorena, an old and new friend now living in Paris, takes me on a fantastic promenade through the Jardin Des Tuileries. After having a glass of red wine at a café inside the park, we decide to sit by a fountain, circled by lounge chairs. Only in Paris. We spend at least an hour watching children sail small boats in the water with ducks swimming alongside. Every now and then, Lorena or I comment on a little something about our surroundings.

Lorena notes, "The ducks look like giants." I laugh. She takes photos. It is one of these perfect do nothing/ everything days. Lorena says that we're experiencing *flâneur* today: "People who walk the city, with no direction in mind, in order to experience it."

While lounging and contemplating the clouds, our navels, the beauty of our surroundings, I feel something whiz behind me. "There she is!" I whisper loudly to Lorena. We had already talked about the people, sights, and sounds of our respective *arrondissements*. The pink lady does not disappoint; she is still dressed in her pink cape, pink hair ribbons, and two-toned heels, with her platinum-blonde

MICHELLE A. GABOW

coiffure matted to the wind. I turn my head and catch her eye as she circles the pond in fast motion.

"Did you see that? She winked!"

Lorena points out that this could be my vivid imagination and a little red wine at work. *Peut-être* but…

The last sighting happens on my last Tuesday in Paris. It is a week of lasts. There she is, climbing up rue Blanche, bicycle in tow. Odd that she is walking instead of riding on this cool, "mostly cloudy" day in Paris. I really want to snap a photo, but she walks at record speed. She magically stops across the street, as if posing for a photo, as if reading my damn mind. I scrounge like a madwoman around my bag searching for my pink Canon to capture this amazing moment, until I realize that it is still luxuriating on my living room chair. When I look up, the pink lady waves in my direction. I check behind me, but there's only the blackboard menu. When I turn toward her, she is already up the hill on her way to the Moulin Rouge.

I finish my café crème and here she is again, walking down my side of the street, tying her bike with the pink ribbon from her hair to a pole. I am flabbergasted, but even more, alarmed when she sits at the P'tit at the table next to mine. I automatically nod to say hello, but she turns her face in the most French of attitudes.

I am deciding whether or not to exit this little scene. I have an irrational fear of people who are certifiably crazier than me. Thank God, my phobia doesn't have a chance to crop up too often.

"*Asseyez… asseyez…*" she commands to no one.

Like an obedient dog, I stay in my seat.

She orders some *fromage* and café espresso but still does not acknowledge my presence. While throwing a piece of

GOD IS A DOG

bread on the ground under her table, she finally glances my way. *"Pour le chien."* She smiles coquettishly. "Sinatra."

"Comme le chanteur," I throw in. I decide that if I'm in this, I'm in it all the way. These are, after all, my last days in Paris. And besides, invisible or not, she has a dog, and after two months, the lady in pink is actually talking to me. Sort of.

"Il est mort, vous savez."

"Quel dommage," I reply. I think that she means the singer?

Suddenly, as if out of an old movie, "That's Life" bubbles out of the café. There is music to her madness. Pink Lady turns to me, as if to explain, *"Pour Sinatra... et pour moi, bien sûr."*

My favorite waitress, Marie, brings me another *noisette* that I didn't ask for and gives me a conspiratory wink. Lady in pink has her eyes closed, mouthing the words to the song. I don't want to but can't help but stare. "What a character," I say to myself.

"Did you say something?" the lady asks.

"No."

"I thought you did."

"You speak English," I say, a little stunned.

"I speak everything!" she exclaims as she rolls a small ball of cheese and dramatically lets it drop from her fingertips for Sinatra.

"We must feed our dogs well. Yes?"

I just nod. I surprise even myself by tearing off a piece of bread and offering it to Sinatra. "Catch," I hear myself say.

"Good boy," she congratulates. "Good girl." She looks directly at me and raises her eyebrows, which open her large, blue eyes. They are smiling. "My little spirit catcher," she adds and appears to pet Sinatra under the table. She encourages me to do the same. "He won't bite."

I reach out to pet him, and I swear I feel something more than air. I want to pull out my notebook and favorite fountain pen, but I resist.

She looks straight ahead but is clearly speaking to me. "We are all spies, we the poets, the outcasts." Then she looks right through me. "You will remember every line."

"Okay," I say. "I need to ask. Are you some kind of mind reader?" I'm a little nervous about asking a direct question. It doesn't quite fit into our conversation—if, in fact, that's what this is.

"Of course I am," she states matter-of-factly.

I think that this is going well; I might as well ask another. "*Je m'appelle Michelle. Comment vous-apppelez vous?*" I reach out to shake her hand.

She not only withdraws her hand but also sits on both hands like a stubborn child, and remains silent for a few minutes, which feels like hours.

"Anonymous," she clearly declares.

"You call yourself Anonymous?"

"I'm sure you must have read much of my work." She bursts out laughing. At first, I feel that I am the butt of her not-so-private joke. But after a few seconds, I, too, am laughing.

The lady in pink is charming. She raises her coffee cup and toasts. "Let's drink to our work." We click coffee cups.

Again, there is silence. She is deep in thought. Her eyes close. It's as if she is dreaming right there in the café. Her lids are moving as they would in REM sleep. She speaks, but her eyes are still shut. "We need them close."

"Who?"

GOD IS A DOG

Her eyes open wide, but she faces the street. *"Les chiens. We need them close."*

I am the one who is now silent. I have a quick, but profound, missing of Stanley, my Yorkshire terrier.

She continues. "Or else the nightmares of life will plague us, as if carved on our bodies, a tattoo of despair."

"Wow," is all I can say.

Anonymous laughs and appears to pick up Sinatra. She places him on my lap. "Let me get a photograph." She obviously remembered her camera. Snap. She adjusts her seat. Snap. Then stands in front. Snap. Bends low to the ground. Snap.

She pulls out an envelope and gently removes its contents, moves my coffee and condiments to her table, and displays many of the photographs from her envelope on mine. One by one, she lays them out, choosing carefully and placing some back in her envelope. She rearranges them several times until, "Voila!"

I pick up one at a time for a closer view before returning them to their place on the table. They are absolutely amazing. The photos are of pierced young women; transvestites; bearded, longhaired men; prostitutes; street characters; older women with lots of makeup, flaming dyed-red hair and painted eyebrows; artists of every shape and form. They are sitting in cafes, in front of the Moulin Rouge, in parks, le Jardin de Tuileries, in front of Le Louvre, the back streets of Montmartre, sex shops, bars, and street corners. In each one, the character is posing with Sinatra, sitting, bending down to pet him, walking him, cuddling him close to breasts and cheeks, lifting him up above the head carrying him like a baby. Apparently, Sinatra isn't very large.

MICHELLE A. GABOW

"Wow!" I say again. My vocabulary is freakishly limited.

Her smile is the fullest yet. Many teeth are missing. Yet, her beauty is unmistakable. "I find myself in every corner of Paris." She is still smiling.

"*Moi, aussi.*" I don't know why I'm speaking French. It just seems somehow truer to the moment.

Lady collects her photos, places them back in a very full envelope, sits, picks up Sinatra, and holds him close to her. When she puts him down, she says, "Sometimes, it's a decision between madness and security."

"Oh, come on. Life isn't that black and white."

She looks through me, as if I have no skin, as if her eyes have a direct line to my blood, my heart, my lungs, my brain, and most of all, my intestines. I feel a churning in my stomach.

For the first time, Lady raises her voice in anger. "*Vous savez. Absolutement. C'est vrai. C'est la vie.* That's life."

"I feel a little sick... nauseous," I tell her. "Maybe it's the coffee?"

We sit quietly. It passes. She knows.

"No, no, no, Sinatra. Not on the table leg. Bad boy." And then to me, "He's such a dog."

We sit in a fresh and new silence between us. Yet, it feels familiar to me as an artist. People pass. We are all in this scene together. One photograph.

The lady in pink breaks the silence but not the thought. She and Sinatra rise to leave. I notice for the first time that there is a basket on the bicycle for him. She kisses me twice on each cheek. I am touched.

Then Anonymous, with Sinatra in tow, swiftly peddles her pink bicycle up toward the Moulin Rouge, leaving me with a trail of Parisian fairy dust and the bill.

JULES ET JIM

by Jim Martel

The world thrives on endless possibilities.

MICHELLE A. GABOW

This is what I do. Well, what I did, then didn't, and now do again. I was stuck and pissed off and so damn lonely. I was living my life holding my breath just to get to my dumbass job. But my art, my real life in a cartoon, was dead to me. I had quicksand for a brain and I was buried in it, along with my aunt, the only person who ever loved me. Grief does that.

So, I took Aunt Rochelle's college fund and skipped town and the States. I hated my first year of college anyway. It was all about dissecting; creative thinking, let alone cartooning, was absolutely out of the question. It took one semester for me to realize that I was also out of the question. My learning curve is pretty high. And, I never much identified with being American. In fact, I felt there was something pretentious and downright mean about patriotism.

Why Paris? I don't really know. Or maybe I do. I was brought up on Godard, Louis Malle, Brunel, and Truffaut. Aunt Rochelle had a knowledge and love for French film that was unparalleled. It was her dream. Her way of living a life of seduction and romance. Her ashes that I flew with me in a small, leather pouch around my waist. Damned if we couldn't finally take this trip together.

To my own astonishment, I immediately got a job under the table in a fancy French restaurant in the *septième arrondissement* known for its fish dishes and inflated prices. I was the "American" busboy, their pride and joy. Almost as easily, I found a room for rent (on the board at the Sorbonne) and a perfect situation; my roommate/landlord spent most of his time away on business. What business exactly, I couldn't tell you. My fantasy was that he was some famous French underground agent. Probably, a computer programmer was closer to the truth. It was a walk from my room in the *neuvième* to the *septième*. And truth be told, walking the streets of Paris was the best part of my job and life, especially the walk home, where Aunt Rochelle and I were continuously in awe of the beauty of the Seine and the mirrored images of L'Arc de Triomphe. Paris was a fantastic installation. And on the way out of the way to home, Aunt Rochelle and I would always have a café crème at a new *brassière* and read and dream at the antique bookstalls.

I was happy for my Aunt Rochelle. After all, she was seeing her Paris. But I was painfully lonely for her at the same time. Life was a ping-pong ball between beauty and grief. There wasn't room for anything else. Cartoons were dead. Art was on hold. Playing with life was out of the question.

This went on for six months until…

MICHELLE A. GABOW

I was suddenly seized. The pencil in my ear, a force of habit, drew it right on a dirty napkin on my tray, a napkin saturated with thick, spicy, garlic clam sauce. I saved it in my blank journal, which will forever have the scent and taste of that moment. I *kinda* like smellin' the flash of inspiration, especially when I'm really far into it. All beginnings have a scent; my beginning lingers.

Sometimes love takes us by surprise.

GOD IS A DOG

Over and over again, we need to unearth enchantment.

Michelle A. Gabow

Life is often in the pause.

God Is a Dog

God is in the pasta.

MICHELLE A. GABOW

My Aunt Rochelle used to say, "There are these unique doors in life. We walk through them all the time. It's only when we look back do we realize that it's a magic door, because it's not the door that opens; it's us. However, our job is to walk through it without knowing where it leads. That takes courage."

(I should note that Aunt Rochelle would always remind me that she took me in through the magic door.)

I never saw myself as a courageous guy. Well, maybe Paris was that step in the right direction to no direction. And most definitely, this older woman and her dog. I don't know who opened our door. It could've been me. Or her. Or the dog. I guess the important thing is the door opened.

Wide.

At the end of my shift.

The woman, dressed in all black with a bright-red scarf, and her miniature poodle, also black with a matching red scarf, had just been seated. I put my backpack on and was about to exit when I heard someone call me.

"Boy. American boy. You can't leave yet!" The woman called in a heavy Parisian accent.

I turned around and *kinda* pointed to myself.

"Of course, you."

"My shift is up," I mumbled.

"I'm deaf as doorknob," she loudly announced and signaled with her hand for me to come over.

When I approached her table, she just stared at me. So did her poodle. I could see the whites of his shifty eyes. Under his breath, I heard a growl as his top lip slightly rose to expose his two molars.

"Join us," she commanded.

88

GOD IS A DOG

No way. I stuttered a bit, "G-G-Got to g-g-o." I hated being forced to speak.

"In that case, we're finished here. You can walk us home." She took my hand so I could help her up. "And besides, I want to see what's in your big black book."

Was she flirting with me?

Then she winked, grabbed my arm into hers and handed me the leash. We walked slowly down Avenue de la Bourdonnais.

As if reading my mind, she told me, "I could walk faster, *vous savez*. But then I would miss all the shifts and changes, gifts for the nose. Close your eyes. Don't worry; I'll guide you. What do you smell?"

I sniffed. "P-p-peaches and bananas."

"And now?"

"Fresh s-s-spices. B-b-basil, garlic, cumin."

We walked a bit, even slower, and I believe made a right.

"And now?"

"M-m-musty… leather. Old b-books."

"Bon, bon!" she exclaimed. "*Mon Dieu*, we've never been formally introduced. *Comment vous appelez-vous?*"

I paused a bit because I wanted to get it out in one fell swoop. "Jim."

"*Mon dieu, mon dieu,* " she screamed. "*Geem! Geem!*" she yelled even louder.

"Oui." We were now on Avenue Rapp.

She pointed to her poodle, who had stopped growling and was now walking like a prince. "You are the *Geem* to my *Gewle*. And I am *Catereene*."

"Truffaut." I stated.

MICHELLE A. GABOW

"*Oui*, Truffaut. *Vous savez. Bien sûr. C'est magnifique*! We have been waiting for you a long time, *mon ami*. How does such a young man know Truffaut?"

"M-m-my Aunt Rochelle re-n-n-named me after Jim from J-Jules *et...* Jim."

"Where is this wonderful aunt now?"

I pointed to my pouch.

"*Très tragique*. We have to sprinkle her on our favorite spots in Paris."

"N-n-no! M-my aunt stays here."

"I disagree. I *tink* that any aunt that names you after Truffaut's *Geem* needs to stay in *Paree*. You can always visit. Sprinkle a little at a time. It's no good all at once. Let's just backtrack a bit, shall we."

We all walked backward, even Jules. I was tripping over the heels of my big feet. They were totally graceful. "You two have done this b-b-backwards thing before."

"*D'accord*, sometimes slow is not slow enough." Catherine stops and tells me to close my eyes again. "What do you smell?" she asks.

"Old books again."

"Yes, you liked that smell. Did Rochelle like old books?"

"Yes."

"*D'accord*. Open your eyes. See that tree? Dust just a *leetle, leetle*. And every time you *visitez* this *librairie*, you can say hello to aunt Rochelle, who is now looking everyday at her favorite *librairie*."

I don't know why. But suddenly, I thought that was so cool. After I sprinkled, Jules, almost on cue, peed. I was about to object but Catherine chimed in.

"He is anointing your aunt. Now she will be forever mixed in the Paris soil of this tree."

GOD IS A DOG

I felt a tear slide sown my cheek. Jules started jumping up and down, until I bent down to pet him. When I did, he jumped up and licked my cheek. Maybe that's when I fell crazy mad for both of them. My first loves in Paris. And right in front of Aunt Rochelle.

We began walking forward when Catherine stopped. "Are you smelling?" I asked.

"What?" she said.

"Are you—"

A middle-aged woman with a child came up to us.

"Catereene, vous et votre ami sommes…"

She gave me a look—a sneer, really, as if I was some con artist just waiting to get my hands into Catherine's pockets and steal everything she owned or ever would own.

"… perdu?," she asked. *"Permettez-moi de vous présenter à votre appartement."*

She and her whining child walked us to 42 rue Sedillot. She went through Catherine's pocketbook and found the keys. I really didn't think that was necessary. She opened the door and gave me another one of her miserable looks.

"Si vous besoin de quelque chose…" she said, and then, in perfect English, all for my benefit, "I'll be right upstairs."

When she left, I gave her the "fuck" forearm. Catherine laughed. Her laugh was full and from the belly. At times, when her hilarity continued, she would snort, which would make her even more hysterical. It really wasn't all that funny but her laughter was contagious. We just stood in the middle of her apartment laughing while Jules chased his tail and barked. We were a goddamn chorus.

Catherine grabbed my hand and pulled me toward a large floor-to-ceiling window. Her apartment was on the

91

MICHELLE A. GABOW

first floor and faced the street. Black corduroy curtains were at its edge, and it felt almost regal.

"I'll miss this."

"What?" I quickly retorted.

"I may have to leave someday, but never mind that." There was a long pause. "Now, why are you here again?"

"You wanted to see my big black book." I pulled my book out of my backpack.

"*Comment vous appelez-vous?*"

"Jim?"

"Oh, *mon dieu*. This is *Gewles*. I am *Catereene*. We have been waiting for you… what's that you have in your hand?"

"M-m-my black book."

"*Mais bien sûr*, it's such a big black book."

Again, the same words, and again with the flirtatious behavior. I was feeling a little confused.

"Well, what are you waiting for? Show the inside."

I started to fumble. I hadn't shown anyone my cartoons except Rochelle. And these, well… these were all about her and Jules.

"There is no time for patience," she announced, which was really more of a demand.

I held my book open on my left forearm, so I could turn the pages with my right hand. We stood side by side, facing the window. A pool of light came through, shining on each cartoon. Catherine noticed and laughed. "The hand of God."

Catherine had several reactions as I turned the pages. At first, she smiled ear to ear, then she began to giggle and laugh out loud, and on the last cartoon, she held her hand to her heart and patted it.

"*Très belle*—" she began.

GOD IS A DOG

I cut her off dismissively. "Well, b-b-beautiful is not a w-w-word I would use—"

"They are quirky and playful. Full of spirit and life, *gewst* like you, my *Geem.*" She planted a long, soft kiss on my left cheek.

I felt my throat swell. I didn't know how to respond and ended up whispering, "I stutter."

"Yes, you do."

That was that. I stutter like I laugh; I cry; I talk. No different to Catherine's ears.

We stood by the window in a holy suspension of time. My hands and face felt warm, touched by the sun and Catherine. It was a present reminder that I am, in fact, a warm-blooded animal. Kinda weird that we need to be reminded now and then.

The silence was pierced by an old and haunting question. "So," Catherine threw into the pond, like a heavy stone, "your aunt raised you. Where were your parents?"

My response was as robotic as it had been each and every time the question was posed. "I never really knew them. They overdosed when I was two… on crystal meth. Aunt Rochelle found me days later on the living room floor of the apartment, with my parents lying in the kitchen. I was barely alive."

She gasped, closed the fist I had no idea I was making into her hand, and stared at me for more than a few moments.

"I love your Aunt Rochelle."

I kissed her hand. Really, I did. And I don't know why. I was an open portal. It was more than a door that opened; it was the skin of our minds.

93

MICHELLE A. GABOW

She told me stories of her life. Each one began with, "It was *tze* love of my life…" She had so many loves and I had never had a one. Well, maybe until now.

Aunt Rochelle always used to say that Paris was the city of romance and seduction. Catherine set the stage, and the curtain was already open. Catherine's last story, the one I remember most, was really her first chronologically. I know she arranged it that way on purpose. Everything, every story, seemed to be designed for our stage.

The lighting was flawless. It flooded both her and me in our theater by the window.

"It was *tze* love of my life."

However, Catherine punctuated this story with two extra words: "*Absolutement! Coup de foudre!*" She paused, as if the memory whisked her away. It was a long pause, but not a silence.

The story, as if unbroken, continued. "His name was Claude. He looked very much like you. Tall. Lanky. Expressive. His black hair was a dark, deep lake cascading down *hees* back with ripples of the crescent white moon sparkling through. No tattoos like you. *Zat* was not the style. He had a large German Shepherd, *Gewles*. Like my *Gewles*, who was always by his side."

As if on cue, Jules came to my left side and sat more like his namesake, the German shepherd, than a poodle.

"Ahhh, but when they walked—no, glided—into *tze* classroom studio, the room opened."

I felt myself grow taller as Jules and I glided around the room, into the darkness and back into the light.

"Yes, my dears, yes." Catherine sang while she lifted her hand into mine and joined us in the dance.

94

GOD IS A DOG

I had never danced with a partner before. In the beginning of our wacky waltz, I most definitely led. Then, somewhere in the middle, it switched to her lead. But in the throes of our waltz, there was no leader. Our bodies followed our minds. We danced as one. In the darkness of the center of the room, we were at the beginning. In the darkness of the center of the room, Catherine was young. The lines of her face faded until there were none. Her hair had the hue of chestnuts. And her body was as light and free as a seventeen-year-old's. I found myself dancing closer and closer, until we embraced and stayed that way. I had never felt closer to anyone in my whole life, even Aunt Rochelle. It took me a second to realize that Catherine was pulling away.

"Come *weet* me to the light," she said.

"No, Catherine, I want to stay here. Why can't we stay here?" I was whining.

"My beautiful man," she whispered, "it ees very sad."

"Why do I have to let go? I like it here."

"Yes, you said to the class that day. This is what theater looks like; it's a dance without a leader. We become one organism, one mind. We are prepared to enter the void, the mystery, together. What a theater teacher you were. What a lover!"

"Yes, I-I-I…"

"I know. You are older; you want me to have your children. *Eeet* has been ten wonderful years. I don't want children. I am not interested in being a mother. I love our life. But you will grow to hate me. I can see the seeds, *mon amour.*"

"No, no. I could never…" I objected.

She touched my lips. Her fingers were cold but soft. Then Catherine pulled her hair back in a ponytail and tied

MICHELLE A. GABOW

it with one of the scarves she was wearing. She appeared younger than ever, even in the late-afternoon light. Even by our window.

I had never felt such a burst of energy in my body before. It was like my body couldn't contain it. My fingers felt tingly and my arms electric. "I love you!" burst out of my mouth.

"Ahhh, *mon amour*. Love! Love! There is *no ting* like it. But sometimes, lovers only see what they want to see. Rapture is a veil *magnifique*! Look around you, *mon amour*. What do you see?"

Almost magically, the room lit up. It was as if there was a light switch at Catherine's fingertips. Click! I hadn't noticed that there was not a stitch of furniture in the whole room. Only boxes. Many, many boxes.

As if reading my mind yet again, she said, "My life is not this room, but it is here. Now. You and *Gewles* gave me that when you glided into my life."

Suddenly, a loud horn came from the window glass and the front door opened. The fucking asshole upstairs was moving her mouth and saying something in French. I noticed that the hardness in her eyes disappeared and there were tears running down her cheeks.

They were talking to each other but I didn't understand a word. Catherine looked awfully confused.

Finally, she asked to no one, "*Pourquoi?*"

"What is happening?" I screamed to the neighbor and then to Catherine. "What is happening?"

"You must really learn your French, my boy. Life is empty without the language of love," Catherine gently commanded.

"What?" Now I was baffled.

"It *ees za* taxi… her cab," explained the upstairs neighbor.

Catherine shrugged her shoulders, as if all this commotion had nothing to do with her.

"I'm going with her, " I told the upstairs woman. I looked at Catherine. "I'm going with you."

"Ahhh…" Catherine exclaimed and then kissed me on the cheek. "How *galant*." Her next words were uttered as if she just remembered where she just placed her long-lost favorite pen. "I'm going where forgetting is a way of life. I will no longer be a foreigner in my own country. " She smiled, and with that smile, her whole body lit up. "Together, we remembered the waltz *extraordinaire, n'est-ce pas*."

Catherine picked up Jules and placed him into my arms. "*Gewles et Geem*," she finally whispered and caught me off guard as she tongue-kissed me, sexy and slow. We stood, Jules and I, by the window long after the cab pulled away.

Michelle A. Gabow

GOD IS A DOG

ABOUT THE AUTHOR

MICHELLE A. GABOW IS A playwright honored to be named the Roxbury Repertory Theatre's playwright laureate in 2011. She lives in Jamaica Plain, a dynamic neighborhood in Boston, with Stella (her ornery but wise cat), Stanley (her inspiration), and her love, Michelle Baxter.